The Erotica Project

The Erotica Project

LILLIAN ANN SLUGOCKI

AND

ERIN CRESSIDA WILSON

CLEIS PRESS

Published in the United States by Cleis Press Inc.,
P.O. Box 14684, San Francisco, California 94114.
Printed in the United States.

Cover design: Scott Idleman
Cover photograph: Phyllis Christopher
Book design: Karen Quigg
Photographs: Marc Travanti
Cleis Press logo art: Juana Alicia
First Edition.
10 9 8 7 6 5 4 3 2 1

Available on CD from TheEroticaProject.com.

To Our Mothers:
Lois and Lottie

CONTENTS

Part III. Cinderella, Pretty Cinderella

Part IV. Sex at Nineteen

Part V. Wet Dreams

Part VI. Don't Move

Part VII. When I Kiss You, Your Mouth Is Filled

Preface

The Erotica Project was created by Lillian Ann Slugocki in her living room in February 1997. In September 1997, she was joined by Erin Cressida Wilson and John Gould Rubin. Together, Erin and Lillian wrote and produced, and John directed and produced, award-winning radio broadcasts on WBAI in New York City. They went on to two critically acclaimed off-Broadway shows at HERE and at Joe's Pub/The Public Theatre. This book contains material from the radio and theater productions as well as new material written for this publication.

Special thanks to John Gould Rubin, director of all the radio broadcasts and staged incarnations of *The Erotica Project;* our literary agent, Andrew Blauner of Blauner Books; and George Lane for his tenacity and loyalty. Deep gratitude and love to the acting talents and friendship of Christen Clifford and Kit Flanagan, as well as the continued inspiration of Sean San Jose and John C. Mackenzie.

Additional thanks to Beth Blickers; Allison Boyer; Douglas Davis; Peter J. Davis; Frédérique Delacoste and Felice Newman of Cleis Press; Patricia Dunnock; Florence Falk; Matthew Finch, director of arts programming, WBAI (99.5 FM, New York); Erica Gould; Hawthornden Castle; HERE; Morgan Jenness; Joan Johnston; Ron Lasko of Spin Cycle Publicity; Julia Lazerus, our research assistant; Kristen Marting; Charles McNulty; Bonnie Metzgar, National Federation of Community Broadcasters; Laura Wallace Rhodes; Nancy Rose, Esq.; Stephen Shainberg; Dixie Sheridan; Julie Smith; *Theatre Forum Magazine;* Marc Travanti; Allison Zell; and the cast, crew, and designers of *The Erotica Project* in all its incarnations.

The Evolution of *The Erotica Project*

LILLIAN ANN SLUGOCKI

I began writing erotica in 1995, the summer my ten-year marriage ended. In the absence of sex, I began to write about sex. I never planned to make any of this writing public. It was too dangerous because I had never seriously mapped the emotional terrain of my own sexuality. As a married woman, sex was domesticated. As a newly single woman, sex was a complete mystery to me. I knew what I liked, but what it meant to me after my lover crept out of my bed at 5:00 A.M. was another story altogether.

Although I was raised as a good Catholic girl in a small Midwestern town, I rebelled instinctively against the tenets of that faith. Particularly Eve, who, in her quest for knowledge, brought about the fall of Man. "Sex is bad; knowledge is bad." I didn't buy the idea then, and I still don't. But it created major repercussions within my sexual worldview. The madonna/whore dichotomy is still burned into my brain. Girls who slept around were bad girls, and there was no getting around it! Not in the Midwest, not in the seventies! Girls like me were forced to pull on pantyhose and a polyester navy-blue dress from Penney's or Sears in the morning and attend a stifling, suffocating Sunday Mass. Often I had to grab makeup to cover hickeys on my neck and endure hangovers and an overwhelming sense of shame in the House of God, our Father. Well, I decided, he's not *my* father.

And there were other images of my adolescence, images that titillated and confused me...the album cover of the soundtrack of *La Dolce Vita:* a whore with scarlet lipstick, her large breasts spilling out of her too-tight jersey. There was the album cover of Herb Alpert and the Tijuana Brass: a naked, beautiful woman emerging from a mountain of whipped cream. And then I found a secret cache of pornography in the garage: shamelessly naked women, grainy and dirty and sexy! And never any discussions about sexuality at home. I was told only the correct way to insert a tampon—but what about a boy's fingers? How come nobody told me how good that would feel? I kept myself safe from all these discordant images, mixed messages, and shame by being a good girl, by staying in long-term relationships, by being faithful, by liking sex but not loving it. I loved my man and I loved my home, but I didn't love sex.

One year after my marriage ended, my mother died. I liken those early days of great loss to the Hanged Man card in my tarot deck. Like the Hanged Man, I was not able to completely comprehend what had happened. Strung up and strung out by grief and loss, I only knew I had to keep writing, because that's what would save me. The writing of erotica became part of that long and arduous—but unbelievably exciting—process of individuation.

Shortly thereafter, I discovered the healing power of sex. And it was intoxicating. He was muscular and passionate, and he never asked me how I was dealing with the death of my mother. This was a relief because I knew I would never fall in love with him, set up housekeeping with him, spend Christmas with him, or introduce him to my family. Never. It was a very simple equation: The way he spread his body over my body made me feel alive. And it felt important, as a writer, as an artist, to continue to create this voice, this persona, to map the sexual awakening of a woman in her late thirties.

By winter 1997, those solitary journal entries written during the "blue hours" between midnight and 4:00 A.M. had grown to include stories I had heard from my friends, stories inspired by conversations floating by me on the F train at 2:00 A.M., stories inspired by dreams, fantasies, photos—in short, by anything and everything I heard and saw. I created a body of work that was a compendium of the voices of different women, in different circumstances, with different life stories—some confessional, some playful, some ironic, and some purely sensual.

I convinced Matthew Finch at WBAI Radio in New York City to give me a half hour of airtime to broadcast my work. I called it *The Erotica Project*. The first broadcast, in August 1997, was powerful but raw, rough. That September, I invited playwright Erin Cressida Wilson and director John Gould Rubin to collaborate with me. Together we wrote and produced a series of radio broadcasts that later evolved into two off-Broadway theater productions at HERE and Joe's Pub/The Public Theatre.

During the run of our show at Joe's Pub/The Public Theatre, Erin and I sat at the end of the bar. As the lights dimmed, we sipped our single-malt Scotches and held hands. Afterward, I felt reckless, redeemed, ready for action. One night we ended up at a tiny hole-in-the-wall bar in the West Village and danced in each other's arms. Two heterosexual women...well, we had been through so much together. Being naked in a bubble bath posing for press shots seemed like the most natural thing in the world. And then, one year later, we posed naked atop a mirrored Plexiglas bar in the middle of the afternoon, wearing nothing but suede high heels. I fixed her hair and she lent me the high heels. Bad girls on the loose—watch out! I reveled in the creation of that persona, that single woman, writing erotica with her best girlfriend and posing naked.

In retrospect, I have to say that being photographed, either in the bathtub or atop the Plexiglas bar, always felt much more a political act than a sexual one. Actresses and models—young, lithe, and in their twenties—pose naked. Intelligent, serious writers are not photographed naked, ever. Especially this writer, over forty. I was startled, bemused, and then very pleased with my audacity. In many ways, these photos were and are part of the necessary machinery of public relations, but, on the other hand, I believe they say something very serious about *The Erotica Project:* that it is revolutionary for women to take charge of and own their sexuality, that I don't have to pretend to be somebody I am not. That I like my body, all of my body. I like my tits and my ass and I like sex, and sometimes, when the moon is full and the chemistry is right, I actually love it.

On Writing Erotica

ERIN CRESSIDA WILSON

I grew up in a house full of books, and because I was an only child, I was alone a lot. Often, because I had nobody to play with, I turned to the written word, looking for something hidden within those books, something naughty. Which hardback would have it? Which paperback? I was never disappointed, because my father had collected—on his topmost shelf—a library spanning the history of erotica ("academic work," I was told). I would climb carefully onto his swivel chair, step onto the desk, and reach up my hand without looking, waiting to see what came down—anything from *The Story of O* to *I Am Curious (Yellow)*.

Even before that introduction to erotic literature, I was intrigued by magazines in the basement. It is said that women are not typically aroused by dirty pictures. I found that not to be the case as I rifled through stacks of *Playboy* and *Hustler*. Wet, dingy, moldy pages with ripe, pink nipples falling from candy bras; lipsticked babes with blonde hair. These magazines were fascinating and instructive to me.

I was born in San Francisco in the early sixties, surrounded by the sexual revolution. When I was a baby, we lived in North Beach, a block from Caffe Trieste and two blocks from Big Al's, on Broadway, where an enormous billboard showed the stripper Carol Doda with flashing nipples. My parents listened to records of Lenny Bruce and Mort Sahl and brought me to the movies *The Mother and the Whore*, *Last Tango in Paris*, and *Swept Away...by an Unusual Destiny in the Blue Sea of August*. Though my mother always told me to look at the floor when the "naked parts" came on, I covered my eyes and looked through the cracks of my fingers, feeling a pain and a pleasure in my groin that made me want to move to a desert island

and do whatever it was that Mariangela Melato was doing with Giancarlo Giannini.

A childhood friend and I used to jump around on her twin beds wearing her flamenco dresses. To me, her house was sex. The walls of the winding stairs were lined in red velvet. There were pictures of her father in a bullfighting accident on the wall—somehow horrific, somehow exciting. Dozens of cats ran through the house, and occasionally a pet fox scurried by. There were whips and capes on the walls. In the middle of their living room, on a small stage, was a queen-size bed with a heavy curtain around it. This is where my friend's half brother, who was twenty, slept when he came to stay. One night, in the middle of the night—wearing one of my friend's flamenco dresses, in which I had fallen asleep—I walked downstairs, and the curtain in the living room opened. Her half brother walked out, completely naked. He held his hand to his crotch but couldn't fit everything into one hand. I stared, and he stood there. Then I ran back upstairs very quietly, having seen a naked man for the first time in my life.

But nothing prepared me for seeing my first erection, for the feeling of it, for the bizarre thing called "come" flying out of a boy, for the first time a boy put his fingers inside me, for intercourse, and the empty, sad, broken, lost feeling of losing my virginity. For the elixir of kisses, and for making out.

I began writing this material when I was in a sexless, though very loving—and for those two reasons, extremely frustrating and saddening—relationship. I was staying at my parents' house in San Francisco. One night, I was falling asleep in my childhood single bed, a Bill Graham Presents poster of the Grateful Dead and the Jefferson Airplane hanging on the wall. To my right was another Fillmore West poster, of a naked woman in flames. In despair about the lack of sex in my life, and caught in my childhood bed, I began writing my first piece.

What I wrote was ridiculous—a takeoff on straight male erotica, but at the same time, it came from *my* world. Lying in bed, writing, I embarrassed myself, made myself laugh, was vaguely aroused, and felt a great freedom to just write what I've always wanted to express: the voices of women unabashedly telling their sexual tales with no apologies. Articulating sexuality and writing it down are, in themselves, sexual acts. Of course—often, sex is in the mind more than it is in the genitals, breasts, or tongue.

I want to create for the reader what I had as a child: the friendship and the partnership of a book. I used to dream that my lover's face was a book, that I'd turn the pages and step inside it. With a book, you can reach across the night and touch somebody you've never even met. It's about fantasy and imagination. And who is to say that *that* is not more real than the physical world?

The Erotica Project

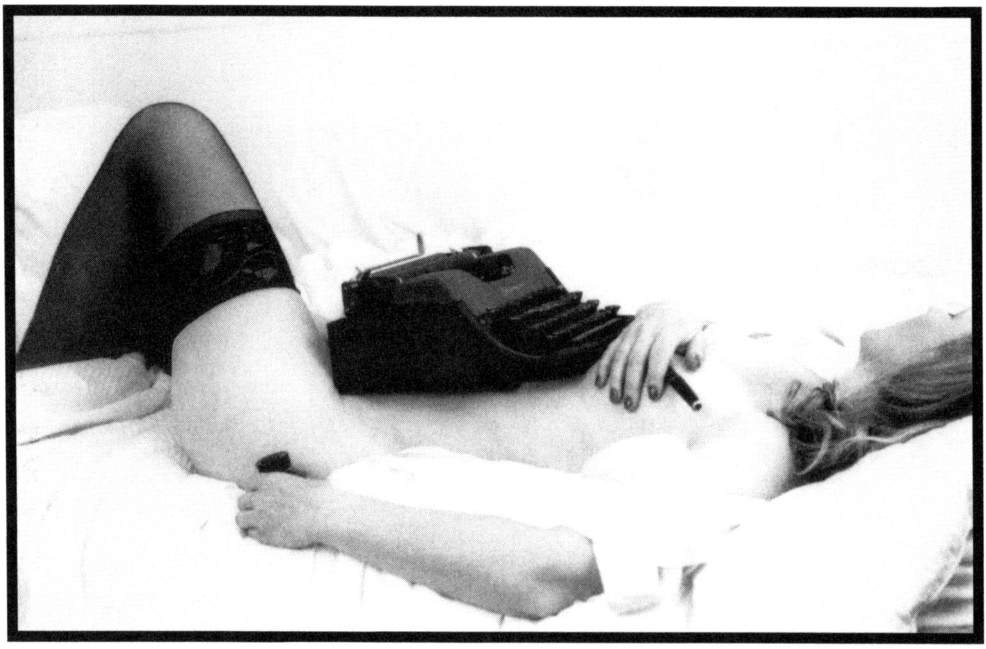

Trash

Alicia wrote pornography. She was living in France and had done well with her erotic novels and had even dabbled in some pornographic modeling, but only while wearing a mask across her eyes.

Her husband, Moss, was British. She had heard of a song that said how good British men were in bed in the dark of night, but that they never made love in the light of the day. This was certainly the case with Moss. The problem was that Alicia didn't screw at night. She needed to see his face clearly and she needed to know that the rest of the world was at work in order to have her pleasure. It was Alicia's desire to take a lover at four in the afternoon. She yearned for an extended hot bath, a long lovemaking, and a nap from which she would awaken at 6:00 P.M. and have a leisurely dinner, after which she would sit down to her writing and a glass of red. But Moss could not face her body, her ass, her tits, her face, in the light. He could not handle her pleasure.

Though Alicia and Moss had opposing sexual tastes, he was her intellectual equal. He had the same sense of humor, the same kind of critical cynicism. She loved to talk to him for hours, and he loved to cook for her. But they never screwed.

Pressing the letters of erotica into her typewriter, Alicia became so aroused that one day she slipped a vibrator under her skirt and sat on it while she typed. Moss sat in the next room, writing his radio plays for the BBC, totally unaware, while the dildo vibrated softly inside Alicia and she squirmed. She'd often come quietly, furiously writing her sentences, sure to place the reveal of the pounding member at the right moment with the dripping pussy: "...and when he entered her and he'd pound her and they'd crash to a screaming orgasm," her fingers screwing the typewriter firmly as her pussy quietly pulsed, held, and released the dildo—a shudder of pleasure rose up her body to her flushed cheeks and she let out one fine quiet breath. Her head fell back and her legs spread indecently.

Her editor told her she put the orgasms too soon in her writing, that she needed to lengthen the narrative and draw it out before the final climax. But she argued with him that she herself always came quickly and then continued to come over and over again. She would write that way, too—with orgasms, or climaxes, throughout the piece. In point of fact, she did not believe in the final orgasm. There was no end to her stories.

Alicia grew to love it more and more, masturbating at her typewriter. But soon the dildo was not enough. On this day, she placed two pieces of paper into the typewriter and began, "Chapter One," a cucumber implanted inside her. She glanced over at the crack in the door. She could see her husband's back, tilting back on his chair, looking out the window, sucking cigarettes, the familiar typing, as she brought her hand down to her calf, stroked up her silk stocking, past her garter, which she pulled at (foreplay and a joke on herself). She opened up her panties, moving the elastic away from herself, and she was already hot and wet. She slipped the cucumber in and moved to sit on it. She felt she would scream, but the secret of the game was to remain calm, to rustle the papers, to look out the window in deep contemplation until the cucumber was all the way inside her. She left it there and began…

Chapter One

The house was on the top of a hill, dark, with only one light in the tower and candles burning, leading the way up the path to the front door. Veronica and Sally were in their first year of junior high school, and they had been given invitations to the castle at recess by a man who had the face of death. Walking up the pathway, Veronica and Sally laced their fingers together. They had kissed before and even seen, touched, and looked at each other's breasts. In fact, Veronica had bitten Sally's breast and Veronica imagined that Sally had orgasmed when she did it. Another time, when Veronica got her period and her mother stood on the other side of the door instructing her on how to insert a tampon, she thought that might be an orgasm, but she wasn't sure. She doubted it. The truth was, neither had ever had an orgasm and were dying to feel one. Veronica and Sally had been familiar with quite a few things, ever since they had gotten their hands on Veronica's mother's copy of *The Joy of Sex* and read it underneath the covers one night, both of them getting hot and bothered. They were twelve at the time and had no idea what to do. So they pulled each other's hair and hit each other until they both fell back exhausted, sweaty, and hot and dropped into a deep, middle-of-the-summer sleep—naked—next to each other.

What was an orgasm? they wondered together. Could you hold one in your hand? Could you hold one in a jar? They were out to capture the perfect orgasm.

So Veronica and Sally rubbed themselves on the knobs of Sally's bedposts. They rolled Earl Grey tea into cigarette papers and smoked that, trying to get high and horny. They took off their shirts and sucked each other's nipples. But no orgasm. They had heard that running water worked, so they went into the backyard in the middle of the day, took off all their clothes behind the house, and took turns turning the hose on each other. Sally plastered herself against the garage door as Veronica sprayed the water at her light-blonde triangle. It felt cold, exciting, and dirty, and Sally squirmed all over the door, but no orgasm. Sally then tried, and she found it exciting to hold the hose on Veronica. What a surprise!

Their final experiment was to stick the hose inside themselves and to turn the water on very lightly. Veronica lay on the grass. The family dog, Bruno, had been tied to a tree. He pulled at the leash, barking the whole time, while Sally placed the head of the hose delicately inside Veronica's virginity. Veronica squirmed a bit in pain. But as soon as the water started to flow, she unconsciously brought her hands to her underdeveloped nipples and started playing with them between her fingers and throwing her head back and forth.

Her toes started to flick wildly as Sally stood by the faucet, ready to turn it up or off as told. Sally liked the feeling of being in charge of the water and found her hand creeping down to her own soft vulva. She unconsciously pressed her hole against the water pump and moved its knob slowly against something she discovered at just that moment—her clitoris! She found that if she moved her hard clitoris very slowly and gently along the cold metal knob, she felt waves of pleasure all the way up through her face. She began to feel something come over her, but just as she began to contract in her pussy, she pushed the knob a bit too hard and the hose spurted out of Veronica's pussy and started flaring uncontrollably all over the ground.

Then they heard Veronica's mother calling out her name, and they ran to the other side of the garage, grabbing each other and crying with suppressed quiet giggles; they laughed so hard they pissed down their legs. The feeling of the hot piss after the cold, cold shower filled them with such a divine feeling that Sally forgot about the mother coming and took Veronica's erect nipples into her mouth and sucked. They fell to the ground into a deep kiss, breathing hard, still unsatisfied. They knew they had to stop quickly, put on their clothes, and run out. Which they did. There, Sally turned off the hose and Veronica ran to her mother to help with the groceries, noting on the way that Bruno, their dog, was still tied up. She let Bruno loose and noticed a long, hard, red erection protruding from him. He jumped up on her leg. She threw him off, looked at Sally, got an idea, and smiled.

Alicia came with the cucumber and pulled it out. She looked through the crack of the door at her British British British husband, who sucked on cigarettes, one after another, in the next room. She wanted to come again, so she moved on to...

Chapter Two...

PART I

Hymns

A Man in My Thighs

Objectify me and I'll objectify you, and that will be our highest form of love. I don't want anything intricate. I don't need S/M, special novel sex, touch-my clit-this-way sex, be sure to screw me only when the scent of rotten apples is filling the bed, make sure that Vivaldi is playing, that the Backstreet Boys are blaring, fuck me with pornography weighing us down on the bed, sit in the corner and dial up a 900 woman who will give you a blow job over the phone, and whack off for me—while you retain a calm voice over the phone, shoot your spunk onto a centerfold, take a bite of steak before making out with me, plant tulips and mangoes and apricots in my cunt and eat them out of me, bronze my nipples and put them in the Smithsonian, cast your torso and let me carry it around as a handbag, open up a small café in my pussy and invite your parents and all your friends over for coffee, look into my eyes and let your pupils dilate as you come and mouth my name—and when you make me come, it's like a house with a goddamn chimney flowing because you are home. All I want is this disease that paints circles under my eyes and keeps me saying idiotic things and empties the career out of my brain and throws feminism out the window with a single thrust, because sometimes I just want to be bent over, thrown down, and spread open and entered and conquered and colonized and nailed. I want to be your property, your nation, I want you to build on me and tend to me. When you're fucking me, treat me like your mistress, your maid, your wife between the linens. I want to write about the one millionth time we made love, in the tenth year of our love affair.

Do You Think We Fuck Too Much?

The night before we are going to part for a month, we go on a date and eat Tom Yum Gung at a Thai restaurant. We go across Wilshire to the department store and look at the sale items as if we are two girls—but you are not a girl. We go into the dressing room, and then you leave it to go find me another size in those pants as I try on a pink undershirt—extra large—on sale in the children's department. The camisole has drawings of underwear: a bra, a tiny tee, a brief, and a demi. I put it on and my tits are big-looking, and you come into the dressing room with your jaw half dropped in an almost stupid sex look. You lift up my shirt and twist my nipples all the way around really hard and ask if it hurts, and I say, "No." Your voice gets lower as you jiggle my tits with your monster hands and then pull my hand down to your dick. You quickly unzip your pants and pull it out, and I lightly feather across the bottom edge of your prick. Then I twist my fingers around it in a circle, gripping the head lightly, and you tell me, "That feels good," as you suddenly descend on me—open-mouthed—and tongue me like a question mark. I breathe heavy and fast—you are strong with your voice getting even closer—as you hike up my skirt and say, "Bend over." I'm bare-legged with clogs and your pants are at your ankles. You're stripping off your shirt because you want to watch yourself fuck me from behind in the mirror. I'm up against the mirror and they have a bar right there, as if they made it just for holding onto while getting screwed from behind in the dressing room of this department store on Wilshire in Santa Monica.

As you push into me, I'm only half wet, and it hurts you and me—and then it's sliding easily, and I look at you as you close your eyes and put your head back, and I think my tits are looking pretty good, better than I knew. You're reaching around to my nipples and mauling my tits from behind as I crane my neck around and we kiss as if this is the most romantic thing we've ever done in our lives, and it is, because you are playing with me and loving me—wandering from room to room, fantasy to fantasy, with no punctuation and no visible transition.

You suddenly pull out of me, put on your sweater, and calmly say—so the customers in the other stalls can hear—"The khakis are a little too big," and I calmly agree with you. You go to try to find another pair. I'm standing there by myself, my hand between my crossed legs, and then I limply put my shirt back on. And now you're back in the stall with a new pair of pants. You hang them up and open your zipper, saying, "Bend over, I want to fuck you again," and we do, as I watch myself in the mirror getting pummeled—we occasionally comment on the fictional thoughts we are having about the clothes we are not trying on. You pull out again suddenly, and as we leave the stall, you buy me a man's crisp white button-down shirt.

We go home and go online separately, watch television, sit on the couch, start fiddling with each other. You say the curtains are half open and that I should close them, but I don't as you climb on top of me and fuck me the way it feels best, and you say, "This is how I like to fuck you before I come on your stomach," and I like you to talk before you come, I like to hear you try to speak clearly, and I can feel the head of your cock getting bigger inside me, and your arms are getting tight, and you've got that look on your face, and it's making me melt. You pull out of me and beat off all over my tits and stomach and ask me—very calmly and quietly—"Do you think we fuck too much?" And I say, "No, I don't think we fuck too much." This is my idea of slippers on the feet, dinner tonight, how was work today, dear. This is the domestic life I've always longed for.

Keep Me Constant to Your Flesh

Darling, darling, darling. Isn't that marvelous, darling? I say, darling, isn't that marvelous? The way your hand brushes up against the fine web of my hair. How casually your arm touches my bare breast. No, don't move. Don't, darling. I say, darling—even if you breathe, if you must breathe, breathe quietly. Like the breath of a bird. The first breath of a bird in the morning. That first breathy breath. That coo. That hum. The way your heart beats when I breathe that breathy breath into your soft moth ears. The way your words syllable into music, the way your fingers turn bone and blood to gold.

I say, darling—don't move your leg. Let it lie here until it is covered in moss. Till the ocean moves across it and lays to rest broken bits of blue glass upon it.

Oh, darling what do I know? What could I possibly know? I say, darling, what could I possibly know?

I know I want you to pin me to the warm earth. Because a body in motion is life in motion. Because your warm tongue is the fountain of the universe. And your arms are gravity. I know I want you to anchor me to the wall of the sky with your long legs and keep me constant to your flesh: the apple of your belly.

Feed me fresh figs from your garden, keep me golden, burnish me with your breath. Take me from the tangled sheets of early morning and deliver me to your body, my darling, and is that enough to know?

I say, darling, are you quite speechless now? Are you quite paralyzed, too stunned to move? Have you ever met a woman like me? My guess, my darling, is that you haven't—my guess is that you are thanking your lucky stars. My guess is that you would move heaven to earth and back again to meet a woman like me. Hmm…there are many ways to show gratitude to a woman like me. I say, darling, there are many, many ways. Time, darling, there is so much time and so much light, and have you ever met a woman like me?

Don't be afraid to flatter your mistress. Please be articulate, please be specific, unabashed—.

You can move now, darling, but you can only move closer. Come. Closer. Here's where we slip into the heart of the morning, here's where we fall into fire. I say, darling, you're quite hot to the touch now: a radiant beauty. You're blushing. You're beautiful. I say, darling—you're quite beautiful.

Tree Frog

My whole hand fits into your palm, my tongue sits in your mouth, my ass fits into your grip, and when you pull your hand away, you leave me with five pieces of evidence, black and blue. Grace says you have fingers like tree frogs', that they are long and spindly with suction cups on the end, and when you bite your nails, you eat them. I bite my nails now to be like you, I move my mouth and pronounce my vowels like you. I roll over and my whole body is made just for you. Pick me up and hold me up to the light, turn me until you find the perfect place to sink your teeth.

The Hanged Man: A Love Story

I smell summer in the high blue air this morning. I smell summer on my skin. I see a mad profusion of red roses. They are not just red, baby, they are scarlet. They fill my blood with longing. My breasts are like roses, they are soft young blossoms, they are lit by fire. I long to fill you with the sweetness of summer, baby. Hang you by one foot from the oak tree, like a prophet, like the hanged man, hang you deep inside my mouth...but I can't find you.

If only I could find you and hang you from the tree in my garden. Cut off your head and keep it in a pretty glass jar, light incense, conjure love potions, sing you to sleep every night. Then I would curl your dark hair, cover it with spiderwebs, and keep you forever. Sing you to sleep like the sirens sang to Odysseus.

And then I would make love to you like Psyche made love to Cupid: late at night, with the moon slung low in the sky. And if I could find you, I would never lose you, but I can't. I can't find you. I am deep into summer and I can't find you, so instead I hang myself on the oak tree, strung up by one foot, upside down. I swing slowly in the summer sky.

I swing slowly and I smile.

The Scar

I'm an impossible wife this way. I'm capable of becoming jealous at the oddest moments, even after I've been weeping for the four straight hours of your surgery. The surgeon said everything looks fine, but I didn't know until I saw you. And when I walked in, the nurse was leaning over you, giving you some morphine. Because her huge tits were in your face and you were looking straight at them—stoned—I got jealous when you kept saying what a "terrific" nurse she was. I remembered my father repeating the same phrase over and over again after his heart failure. And when she left the room, you said, "Come here. Where's my brother, where's Dave?" I said, "They went to eat breakfast." And ten hours after your brain surgery, you grabbed my hand and put it under the sheet, and I cried because you were OK, you could get an erection, for Christ's sake, and in some silly way, that proved that you hadn't lost your marbles. You smiled like a kid thinking he's so great, and the nurse walked back in. I leapt into the chair and giggled high like a girl as the big-breasted nurse administered three more drops of dope for the pain. Your jaw dropped open again. And even though I had just skirted widowhood, I could not stop the erotic bug of jealousy.

I'm Wet

I know you will love my nipples. I know you will love my hips. I know you will love the look of me, naked in your arms. But you've got to call me, darling—otherwise I can't lure you down to the river. Otherwise I can't tease you in a tight T-shirt. I can't open my legs to your fingers. I keep a picture of you between my legs. I picture you between my legs. I say: "I'm wet, I'm wet. I'm drowning, and only you can save me."

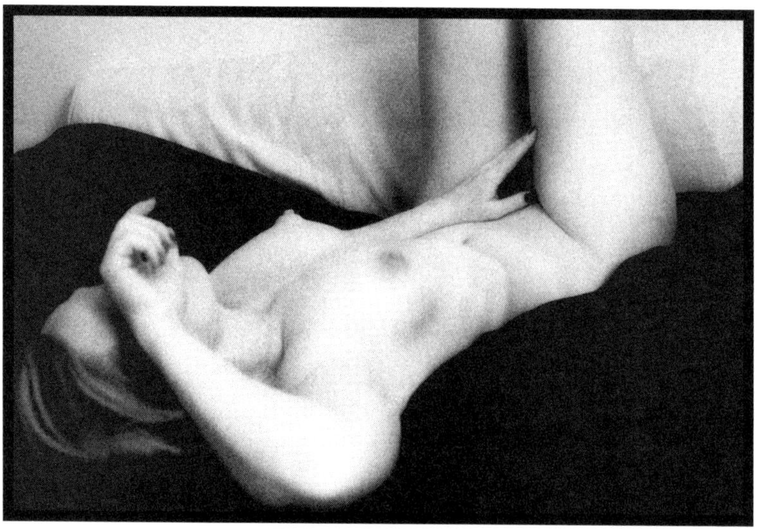

Kiss, Don't Kiss

I pulled the belt loops of his painter's pants toward me, and we hovered our mouths over each other's for seconds, minutes—then hours—as we wanted to make the moment before the first kiss last all night long. He'd asked me to come over to play Scrabble with him. We made big words, flirted, and drank tall boys on his bed in the West Village.

In Particular

Well, darling, we have our brief and particular memories, don't we? In particular, the night I walked home from your apartment: my thighs still damp, my lips rose-hued and bruised, your hands down at the edge of the island and the lush green night....

The brisk engagement of your eyes to my thighs, strong calves. Your hands curling from the kitchen. A smile curling to fit your mouth on the back of my neck. At the bar, you suddenly reached over and kissed me. In particular: a smoky, lazy resonance at the back of your throat, rising over the warm lines of your lips...in particular, on mine....

A lusting, long, thirsty drink. And heavens, darling, I was a thirsty woman. Lusting in particular at the movies: I remember crawling with your tough touch. And then a rainy night, my cheap dress drenched in your smell. Whatever, whatever. In particular, I play with language the way I play this out, the way you play up your heart: tight, no key. And I am too tired and too filled with my particular pain to try. But, here's this:

One bad year. One long good-bye.

My Neck

Hickeys up my neck in the shape of your initials. You kissed your name into me before we left each other. I packed my vibrator and Colette, and you went back and forth, ignoring that I was leaving, then making jokes about it. Then you threw yourself at me and I tried to swallow you whole, to keep you inside me in my travels. That's when you lightly and strongly sucked each letter, in dots—small ellipses of sucked blood—until I was yours.

PART II

Candy Store

Kittens' Tongues

She liked the tongues of kittens when she was in bed. Enticed with carefully placed drops of milk, they would stay there for minutes on end and lap the milk up appropriately. The kittens, and their rough tongues.

Paris

We were spending five weeks in a hotel next to St. Germain that was also a whorehouse. Two double beds for the three of us, and I was thrown in bed with my snoring father because my mother said he kept her awake. My father snored like the ocean. I never knew when the next wave would come, and just as I dozed off, in came another wave to knock me over as my father flipped in the air like a salmon, coming down with his legs and arms stretched out. I clung for dear life to the edge of the mattress. A lifeboat?

This particular night, Paris went on in the dark—the Deux Magots and the clinking glasses—when in my sleep I heard what seemed to be distant crowds, applauding, "oohing" and "ahhing," and then my mother gently hissing at me from across the room. Kneeling before the window, she quietly insisted, "Come over here, come over here, come over here." With red light filling the room, I pulled myself out of my sleep, reluctantly dropped to my knees with her, looked over the edge of the window, and saw below me, on the rue Saint-Benoit, in the bed of a truck, whores dressed as American political dignitaries.

It was George Washington, it was Abraham Lincoln, it was Nixon, and Spiro Agnew, and Kissinger. There were big white wigs and false noses, masks and lipsticks, full breasts falling out of double-breasted suits, lace ascots, and blue velvet outfits, dress shoes and pointed shoes from another century. Blushing thighs and ripe asses emerged from under coattails. Military dignitaries with slits in their crotches and clefts rising up to our window. Open legs and pinkish nipples. It was American men of politics inhabited by a truckload of French whores. It was a truckload of French whores slipped into the skins of American men of politics. Ladies of the evening in costume, up for auction.

But it was the one dressed in the George Washington outfit for whom the crowd gathered, as she opened her legs to the sky. From the terraced window of our fourth-floor hotel room, we could see her glistening, delicate sex. But what was amazing was that this wet and gorgeous cunt was gently clicking. And all eyes focused.

The streets became quiet, the sirens and cars seemed to stop in Paris as if only to listen to the singing petals of her flower. A song. In different pitches came a broken "Star Spangled Banner" as my mother and I huddled by the window, shocked and delighted. My mother took my hand and showed me the ways of the world from this Paris window, as we allowed our gaze to fly out and hover above the crowd. By waking me, she seduced me into the voyeur. With our backs to my sleeping father. That summer night when I was eight, in Paris.

Candy Store

It was 1969, and the candy store was a half block from Grandma's old house. We were a posse: my brothers, my cousins, and I. And we would run in there like idiots for Popsicles and chocolate bars, panting like young dogs, deep in the bright days of summer. But then somebody dropped a bomb on that store and blew it the hell away, and farther down the block, the narrow brick alleyway where Raymond blew his brains away when he came home from Vietnam.

A few months later, my grandparents moved, and I can't say that I blame them. But before the bomb blew up the candy store, and before Raymond blew his brains out, we found a stack of dirty magazines congealing in the shadows of the garage. Our favorite was *Camping with a Cutie*. The "Cutie"—shot somewhere in black and white—was arrayed naked with a stiff blonde hairdo, black eyeliner, and a sad sad smile, and her butt was like a clamshell floating on the surface of a dirty lake. We were agog. Brilliantly titillated, but always, always careful to put them back exactly where we found them.

We wandered back into the house for chips and milk and found our parents arguing in a foreign language over a ten-dollar pot in their ritual poker game. They barely acknowledged us, so we knew we were safe. In the next magazine, *Naughty Housewives*, we found a brunette with a dark beehive vacuuming the house, wearing only an apron. Her large breasts jutted out like a canopy over the rest of her body, her belly swelled over her black curly hair, and she looked at the camera as if nothing was amiss. As if she vacuumed the house every day completely naked save for a tiny, frilly apron. My groin ached, and I wondered in what part of the world ladies took off their clothes for strangers.

I practiced at home, in front of the mirror. I didn't have breasts, so I had to make a brassiere for myself. I ripped apart an old sheet and fastened it together, securing straps and cups with bubble gum. It was summer of 1969, and I kept looking down my shirt to make sure it stayed put. My mother yelled at me from the back door: "What the hell are you doing?"

I didn't answer because I didn't know, but I got the hell out of the sun because the gum started to melt against my skin. Then I tried standing on the edge of the bathtub so I could get a full-length view of my naked body and my new brassiere. I wrapped the clear plastic shower curtain around me. I envisioned myself all grown up, wearing a sexy cocktail dress. I smiled a captivating smile. I showed a shapely ankle. The photographer took my picture and paid me lots of money.

Every Sunday I said, "We're not going to look at those magazines." But even though I was the oldest and knew better, nobody listened. We had stumbled into a strange land and knew we could never go home again and knew we could never stop. Even the lush white peonies growing right outside the garage couldn't help. A couple of weeks later, the magazines mysteriously disappeared and we returned to the streets, panting like young dogs, set loose upon the world again.

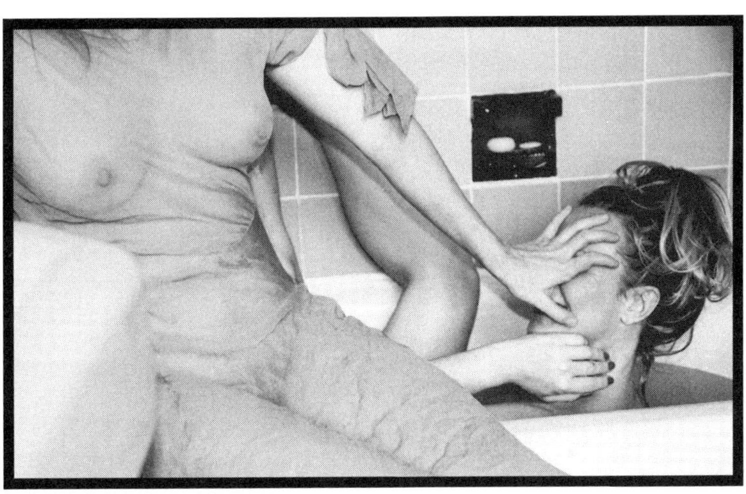

Hand Job

One boy persuaded me to give him a hand job in a deserted railroad car. We climbed up the overpass through dry grass that scratched my flesh. He held my hand. "Trust me," he said. I nodded. He lay on his side inside the car, and I lay down next to him. I blinked to adjust my eyes to the darkness. He gingerly extracted his prick from his pants and put my hands on the shaft. "Just up and down. Up and down."

The Skin of a Leopard

Remember when we would dare each other to eat from the dog-food bag at the edge of your basement and then we'd run to the freezer and you'd show us the raw venison that your father shot? Remember the time we ran all the way upstairs to your dad's attic room where he had trophies from his safaris in Africa?

A stool made of an elephant's foot, bracelets made of elephants' hair—in a bowl—to run your fingers through, gazelle hooves as the feet of a table, and skins everywhere, several severed heads on the wall looking down onto Brooklyn Heights.

When the pelts were brought in, I always thought they were beautiful, silky, full of colors that sprayed themselves across the floorboards and sofas of your attic. I wondered why your mother wasn't jealous. Because these pelts were so sexy. How could she compete with the head of a lioness, the skin of a leopard, the inanimate hide of a zebra?

When I'd leave your house, at five in the afternoon, your father would not be home yet. I would pass the kitchen where your Mexican maid prepared fresh pasta and refused to learn English. Your mother teetered on the corner of one of the pantry cabinets, pouring another Scotch on the rocks, with that special sexy sound—a singing—as the single malt hit the ice. I wondered about your dad—could he compete with that alcohol? And then I saw the war between them, fought with furs and liquor.

Tiger Beat

It was the unfolding of the poster of David Cassidy from the center of the magazine that was so difficult. Because I was in a tight bathroom stall and there were knee-socked girls in middies all around me, I didn't want them to hear the rustle of the magazine paper unfolding as I placed my hand up between my thighs and my Adidas shorts. I'd open up that poster of David Cassidy, and the first thing I'd get a glimpse of was that feathered hair. The shag. I felt it right away, that sour exciting feeling in my lower stomach. Sex. I'd open up the poster and concentrate, at recess, only five minutes left before the bell, my P.E. shorts under my blue skirt—and my Wallabies. With proper concentration, the image of David Cassidy would kaleidoscope into any seventies icon with hair feathered just so…a glimpse of Hoffman, Redford, Pacino. Anybody whose hair was slightly too long. To this day, I am compelled to search out men whose hair reminds me of the seventies, of the rockers—Barry Manilow, Rod Stewart, the Fonz. I am forever filled with those memories against the bathroom stall—coming quietly with my breath against the yellow partition between me and Mary MacDougal—then pulling up my socks to just below my knees, tucking them over once for a neat cuff, and finally folding up the poster of David Cassidy and carefully placing him back between the shots of Leif Garrett and Bobby Sherman. Ouch.

Last Night, under a Full Moon

Last night, under a full moon, I let Fred stick his hands down my pants. And earlier that day I let him stick his hands down my pants behind Andy's garage. I know I shouldn't let him do it, but why does it feel so good? He doesn't even unzip my tight jeans all the way, just halfway, and then he shoves his hands into them. First he sticks one finger inside me, pulls it out, sucks the juice from it, kisses me, and sticks his hand back down there, and then he puts two fingers inside me. And I swear to God I just stand there, wriggling like a little worm caught on a hook with the biggest smile on my face. I know he finger-fucks a lot of other girls in the neighborhood. I know that I am not his main girlfriend, and even though he has my phone number, he never ever calls me. My best friend said, "You're not a slut because in your heart you love him."

And it's true, I do. I dream about him all the time, but when we meet in my dreams, everything is so soft and tender. He calls to me in a low sweet voice, not like in real life, when he says, "Meet me in back of the garage."

In my dreams, he says my name like this: Veerrronnicaaa. Then I hear my favorite song on the radio about loving my man forever. In my dreams, I'm all grown up and beautiful and my tits are bigger, and I'm even wearing a black bra, not this little T-shirt thing. So then I walk over to him, the room is dark and smells pretty, and I sit on his lap, and he kisses me and blows in my ear. And that's all. That's all we do. We just kiss, just so soft. In real life, when he finishes finger-fucking me, he tells me to wait behind the garage while he walks out first. Then I follow, my jeans zipped up and my panties all wet. Then he puts Grand Funk Railroad on his record player and rolls joints. He ignores me.

God, I love him.

After Fred, I kept long lists of all the boys that kissed me:

Billy, down at the beach, his mouth tasting of lake water, his arms burnished by sand and sun. Martin, with his large mouth that tasted like hashish and cigarettes. Keith, the chlorine god, his hair bleached by the brilliant sun. And finally, Joe, Pretty Boy Joe, who crept into my bedroom one night when I was thirteen, who was three years older and tried to penetrate me. But it didn't work because the condom felt like plastic wrap around his cock and, honestly, was there room down there? Some boys bruised my mouth, some boys finger-fucked me in the schoolyard on a Saturday night, some boys grabbed my small breasts and bit my nipples, some boys dry-humped me in the woods at night when the moon disappeared behind the clouds.

After Fred, boys seemed to come from everywhere. Boys who wanted to look down my tank top, boys who wanted to go for walks in deserted parking lots, boys who wanted hand jobs, boys who wanted to stick their long tongues deep inside my mouth, boys who wanted to feel me up after school behind the bakery, who drooled onto me and said, "I love you." Ricky, Tommy, Martin, Jeff, Joe, and Bill. I didn't do it because I liked it; I did it because I knew I had to. But I dreamed of different boys at night: boys I never met, boys I might fall in love with, boys who tenderly took me into their arms and softly kissed my mouth, who carved both our names into old trees in magical forests, who took me sailing on an autumn afternoon when the lake looked like a bright band of silver. Boys who held me and kissed me and caressed me and never stuck their hands down my pants.

This Is What He Told Me

We had a house cleaner named Susannah Sakowsky who—at the time—must have been thirty years old, and she was from Yugoslavia, the former Yugoslavia, now Bosnia.

Susannah had the largest chest I had ever seen in my life, and she wore tight sweaters while cleaning house every week. My dad was at work and my mother was very, very busy. So, Tuesdays were a big event for me, because I was obsessed sexually with Susannah Sakowsky.

I used to go up to my bedroom and set myself in place. She would vacuum the hallway but never our rooms. So as Susannah got to vacuuming outside my room—mine was the third one—I'd casually position myself naked on my bed—I was fifteen—and my hope was that she would come across me with my furious member in my hand and want to come over and suck me or whack me off.

The closer the vacuum sounds got, the more heightened and erotic it got. I'd stand by the partially opened door watching her huge jugs jiggle as she pushed the Hoover back and forth, and I'd imagine that she actually came into my room as I was whacking off. I wouldn't move to cover up, and instead of being shocked or leaving, Susannah would come over to me—without taking her eyes off of me—and undo her bra—this massive corseted bra—and my hands would go from my dick to her tits, and she would hike her skirt up—this peasant-looking, Yugoslavian skirt—and she would sit on my cock. And when I would come, I'd nut all over her fucking huge rack. And each and every Tuesday, I'd be in my room—about one-thirty—and position myself, hoping that Susannah Sakowsky would come in and fuck me.

Christa

In front of me now—swollen—six months with child, Christa. Her face and expressions look exactly the same as they did when we were children together, the smile at the edge of her lips, her voice.

I am fourteen years old again and I want her tragedy, her abandonment, the tears in her eyes on the tip of my tongue. I want her embrace, arms stretched round me in the child's white iron-framed bed, and her mother with tight French jeans leaning into my father's car like a coquette, and the jams and the hams, the glass of red, the café au lait, and the Laura Ashley wallpaper. I want her perfume, and her feet with arches that point for days and days, the cross of her legs, perfectly waxed—even at the age of fourteen—I want the small, light mustache across her upper lip, and her big front teeth that flash when she laughs loudly, and her fingers with rings that look like they will slide off because her knuckles are so thin and dainty, and the white, white edges of her fingernails. I want her espadrilles and her smile again, I want to be feminine like Christa, and I want to walk around in a cloud of Diorissimo from Christian Dior and be able to speak French and serve hot biscuits and a strong cup of coffee that smells like her house.

The Brace

I would take off my back brace and feel unembraced. Scoliosis: curvature of the spine.

The brace went from my chin to over my pubic bone, made of hard white plastic with metal teeth on the back that pierced fabric strips that I twisted about myself and tightened. It held me for four years during adolescence. Like a lover, a home. I would get an hour off from it each day to be free, and by the end of this time, I would crave to have it hold me again. It bored into my skin in a spot that I'd spray with alcohol for a sting that felt good. The brace technician—the man who made false appendages, leg and arm braces—asked me if I would like to volunteer to show my brace to a group of doctors. I said yes. Then he took two Polaroids of me—from the front and from the back—as he did every six months. He placed the Polaroids under tattered plastic in a photo album full of individuals bent so far over to the right that their torsos were almost touching the ground. There were pictures of half-naked men and women with prosthetics. Then he briefly commented on how my breasts had grown and he kept his hands on me too long. What he crafted was what kept me standing up straight, what was my best friend—warm, tight, and secure.

The next week I went to a circular auditorium at the state's university hospital. I walked out on a stage wearing only a white leotard and a brace. I felt ugly and special. And as much as I pulled down the back of my leotard, I felt stripped and open. The doctors in the small amphitheater all wore white coats. You could see my nipples through the leotard. That was pornography. That felt bad. The gaze. The brace, that felt good. That was home—teetering and floating across the stage.

A Tin of Erasers

I'm sick of it. I don't want to hear about it, see it, smell it, feel it, see it in someone else's eyes, sense it in my groin for just one instant. I don't want to see another big-breasted woman in another magazine, I don't want to be inadvertently aroused by an ad, I don't want to have cable TV and have to skip the porno, I don't want to have to avert my eyes whenever I finish a magazine or newspaper because of the flood of sex ads and personals, I don't want to walk by another sex shop, I don't want to see another strip club. I want to think about something else.

I don't want freedom. I want repression. I want my childhood, I want my Catholic school uniform. I want pre-sexual.

This is what I want. Pencils inside pencil sharpeners—the kind from second grade—that are nailed to the wall inside the supply closet. I want a fingernail in my mouth, and the taste of peppermint paste from the large jars that we spooned out with tongue depressors. I want stars at Christmas and pumpkin on my fingers, the taste of mushroom caps floating in my mouth, stacks of notebooks, pages and pages filled with practice sentences in cursive, a tin of erasers, three paper clips, running my hand through a bowl of marbles, and 100 percent cotton sheets in a single bed. I want the sound of voices coming out of church in the distance, the medical cabinets with squeaking creaking iron, stacks of silver, a bowl of colored ribbons. This is the world I want to sleep with, not just some guy I pick up or some blind date. I want to fuck my childhood, not people. I want a kaleidoscope of everything I found delicious as a child, every street, every place, the basketball courts, the smell of eucalyptus at Land's End, and the sound of the Jefferson Airplane practicing above China Beach. All the houses you and I first felt anything in. I want to fuck the view of my childhood beginning, the icon, the French teacher, the rulers, the blackboards, the knee socks, the recesses, the tetherballs, kick-the-can.

I don't like to fuck people I just met. I like fucking people I already know. I don't even really like fucking people I already know. I'd like to fuck this page, the ink, the typewriter, and the desk. The scene outside my window, and the chair I'm sitting on.

PART III

Cinderella, Pretty Cinderella

The Shell

It was his fingers she loved the most, small and strong, perfectly proportioned fingers that slid in and held her like a handle. "Can you come in my hand? Come in my hand, come in my hand."

This seemed a peculiar way to put it.

But she did. She pushed down and produced a tiny shell...a gift. The shell popped out of her and into his palm. He held it and turned it, and moved it in his hand. Later, he took it out and laid it on top of the bureau. And when he left in the morning, he forgot to run his hand along the top of the bureau.

He forgot to take the shell they'd worked so hard to make.

She sat up and watched this happen.

Bourbon Street Blues

I walk down Bourbon Street with him at two in the morning. Revelers paper the street like bright bits of confetti. We stop at every corner to kiss and deeply kiss. I've known him for two hours, but he whispers in my ear, "I think I love you." We come to a quiet café where we slow dance, and his body feels like thick molasses, his arms encircling me like slow smoke. He orders another beer and buys a gold strand of Mardi Gras beads; he rings my neck with them and kisses me behind the ear. He says he is a lucky man. He's foreign and his accent tickles the back of my throat. Strangers tell us we are a handsome couple. We walk back to his hotel, the gold beads swinging between my breasts.

In his hotel room, he comes up behind me, but I play coy. I move away and say, "Tell me about yourself." I notice my reflection in the mirror. I smile because I am so pretty with the gold beads around my neck. Then his arms are around my neck. He turns on the radio and guides me to the bed. We kiss and deeply kiss. My lips have known his lips all my life. Yes. I take off my shirt and my pink brassiere. The gold beads dangle against my naked breasts. I roll up against his fat erection, he draws the beads tight across my nipples, he unpins my hair and pulls my head back.

He whispers, "Cinderella, pretty Cinderella, please stay the night." But I can't. By morning my gold shoes will be tarnished, my hair undone, my lipstick smeared across his pillow, and he will look at me and think, who is she? Even I can't answer that. So I get up and walk around the hotel room, conscious of how pretty my breasts look, conscious of the weight of the gold beads. He watches me from the rumpled bedclothes. I take my time fastening my pink brassiere. I light a cigarette, sway a little to the music, and then pull my shirt over my head. He walks me to the elevator, and while I am pinning up my hair, he pushes up my shirt and kisses my nipples.

Outside, while I am waiting for the cab, he becomes shy and awkward. He boasts about the Armani suit he just bought. I finger the cashmere of his sweater.

As the cab turns onto St. Charles and through the dark greenery of the Garden District, I know I will never see him again. But in a perfect world, we walk hand in hand down Bourbon Street again. Suck down raw oysters and drink sweet rum. Order room service for breakfast so he can butter my breasts and poach my tongue in his mouth. The raspberry jam is very sweet and neatly covers his cock. In a French bakery, we order beignets and chicory coffee. He buys a voodoo doll that he pierces with gold pins so I will never forget him. In a perfect world, I am transformed for all time into a beautiful woman. So beautiful that every morning and every night I enjoy the liquid conspiracy of two bodies. So beautiful that I know for all time the rustle of sheets and damp underwear, and I know, with utter conviction, how smoothly the key fits into the lock.

Mosque

The Mosque in Paris. Her breasts fall on my head and over my face, she's talking in another language, gesticulating and touching me like a god. Making blood run through my veins. She reminds me of George, his hands pressing into me, all around the groin, brushing over my nipples, my pubis, and the cat crawling around his legs. The way his feet were the only thing I could see because I was on my stomach, my face cradled in a hole, but mainly the time with him was all about feeling, receiving his elbows and fingers, because I was living with a man who wouldn't touch me. I would go to George, who would push the blood back into my loins, my heart, my toes, my vulva, "...the multiple heads that arise from the pelvic girdle, the femur, the tibia, the quadratus femoris, the jaw muscles and the tensor tympani, the facial nerves, the ear muscles." And my temples.

These are the words he would use on me as his cat's tail would slap my hand that fell drunken from the table, the fan spinning over my ass and up my cheek. George would make small, quiet noises. The sound of dishes being washed in other apartments on the Upper West Side drifted through the window. He felt my skin as if it were not skin—but sex. He touched me like feathers, like a totalitarian, he slapped me and told me about the book he was writing on the hieroglyphics of pain and the full spectrum of feeling. But I didn't need to be convinced of that—I thought as I rolled over—slow as a slug—enchanted on the tip of his finger. He'd kiss my forehead sweetly and flop a sackful of rice over my eyes.

I'd wake up a goddess. He would be out of the room, a ghost, demon, lover. I'd look in the mirror, straight at my face, relaxed so much it was beautiful—and my body, with no touch of embarrassment, just the whisk of the fan and the heat caressing my thighs.

I'd always fold the check as I left. I slipped it in his hand and descended the five stories onto Amsterdam Avenue.

The Invitation

I have invited a man I hardly know to stay here at my apartment, with me, in my bed, for forty-eight hours. I met him a week and a half ago in another city, and then he called late, late last Saturday, with an erection in his hand, and told me he was coming to visit me. Said I should stop playing tough guy and he would stop playing tough guy and we should both stop playing games and then he jerked off and I felt like I was fourteen years old, wearing knee socks, finding out just how sweet a boy's tongue could be in my mouth. He told me his cock was hard, that he was going to climb on top of me, that he was going to go down on me and eat my pussy and never come up for air. Sweet Mary Mother of Jesus, I was so aroused. And I thought: I don't care how crazy this is. And I thought: I don't care what's at stake, and whether he means it. I don't care if I get hurt.

I hope. I hope he has a big cock that gets very, very hard. I hope he can deliver the goods, go down on me and stay down for an eternity, then come back up for air and fuck me. And when he kisses me, I hope his mouth fits smoothly over mine like a riding glove on a patrician hand. And that when we fall asleep, his body doesn't feel like a foreign body, but a body that cradles my breasts, his tongue in my ear, his breathing warm and deep. I hope.

Last night, when he called, he talked about his neighborhood and how the bats come out at dusk.

I asked, "What about monarch butterflies?"

I asked because once I watched a flock of monarchs sail out over the Hudson River. I watched them for hours and hours. They flew like autumn leaves, they sailed like grace. This week I am an alchemist, spinning heartache into hope and dreaming dreams about bats and butterflies and large erections that swirl out of their dark corners as the sun goes down.

The Middle of the Day

The five minutes before the first kiss, the promise of the tablecloth, the wine, the times. It is in this pure potential, in the moments and days and years before the first kiss, that I live with you.

And on that day when you ran up to my car—as I was leaving town—and you took my chin in your hand like it was yours to keep, you touched your lips strongly to my forehead, leaning into the car, you joked, "People gonna think I'm scoring dope," and you kissed me all over my face in the middle of the San Francisco sun. And then, just as I was about to go, you finally pressed your mouth into mine, and I held your tongue and I accepted your kiss. I felt it in my whole body, and then we smiled like children. You ran to your own car, I drove away to leave town and wept because I had had a year of no love—not even a kiss—and now I knew I could still be entered—even through the lips—after a year of sadness, when my sexuality was taken, when my heart and mouth and sex shut as if never to be opened again, you put your mouth to mine—you hinted to me that I could still love, and you kissed me with experience, innocence. You.

West Fourth Street

What's it like, walking home from your house in the morning? Well, I saunter down Eighth Avenue to Abingdon Square, then cut over to West Fourth. My thighs are damp and my mouth moves over the memory of the way that you kissed me. Yes, you are a very experienced lover. As I stop for traffic, I recall the way your tongue did figure eights over my clitoris. Your mouth deep into my crotch, your hands deep inside me, and yet I am not even close to emotional fulfillment, and this puzzles me. How is it possible to relinquish every last ounce of physical control to you, yet not one iota of my soul? It is a mystery that perhaps will never be solved.

I sit on the couch with you in the mornings in your dark, small apartment crowded with sneakers and newspapers, with a disheveled bathroom, and we drink coffee. Your conversation strays always to inconsequential things. You are guarded and secretive and quite possibly sleeping with another woman. You are a man who can have many, many lovers at one time. A man who would relish another feminine body, another pair of breasts, a new belly, an unexplored head of long, lush hair. I know this about you. I know. As your tongue and your hands and your hips ride over the geometry of my body, I know that you have had many, many lovers. And I know that it is practice that has made you perfect.

Oh, my man, you do not engage your heart when you kiss me. Your emotions, like mine, are locked up like Spanish doubloons far beneath a troubled sea. But I continue to call you. Knowing all this, I continue to spend the night with you, naked and sweating. And it will end in the simple inconsequential way the night ends slowly, gradually, without fanfare, without fireworks. This is what I think as I walk home from your house, away from your charming lips, your strong thighs, away from your skin so much like the skin of an animal, taut and polished. A gleaming blanket for the cold, cold man who lives beneath it. Shh, please. These words might sound bitter, but they are not. Because in the end, you do not know me. Oh, you know my body, and I can say that I have never had anyone disarm it with the same expertise as you. Disarm it and disassemble it like a watchmaker who covets each shining piece of machinery, who polishes each one with a chamois and holds it up to the light with a small smile of satisfaction.

This is you: watchmaker, artisan, lover. Lover of all women. Lover of all things feminine. Lover who opens me up like a child would open my womb, opening fuller like a bitch giving birth to a litter of puppies, like a raw wound. In the face of death and despair, I cannot think of a better, sweeter, more bitter medicine, and I swallow it like I swallow you. With pleasure. Listen: I spent two weeks up in the mountains with you, watching a hawk circle the clear sky overhead, drinking cool water, making love and tending to my body like an indulgent mother, frustrated by accidents, pain, and too many nightmares. Gently, gently, and still more gently. What was it like, you may ask. What was it like?

"It was pure paradise, honey. It was milk and honey, honey. It was watching storm clouds gather in the north sky and parade south over the tops of the mountains. It was coffee at ten and strong hands at noon, and white wine under white stars that cut the black night in two."

The Etiquette of One-Night Stands

It's Saturday night, he's wearing black leather pants, I see him before he sees me, and I know I will be fucking him before the night is through. So we sit together, have a glass of wine. So then he's touching me and I'm touching him. So we stand outside the restaurant and smoke a joint, and then I ask him to come home with me. But then, but then...his six-foot-tall self is in my small apartment and I realize all I really want to do is sleep, but too late, folks! It's just too late.

So we're kissing and we're kissing, so he unrolls my khakis, unpins my hair, so I pull off his black leather pants and his shirt...his modest erection asserts itself against my thigh. So I pull out a packet of condoms. And he enters me, but it's this thing where he doesn't come but he doesn't stay hard, either. And after a while I really want to just sleep. But he wants to keep trying, he tells me he likes it doggy style, so I roll over, arf, arf, and he tries, he really does, but it's just no good, and I'm not wet anymore, and I'm actually feeling a little sore and put out. I wonder if there is a rule book I can consult....

I would like to propose an etiquette of one-night stands: If at all possible, please leave after we make love. But if this is not possible, if it's very late and you are very drunk and you spend the night, please put on your underwear and go home first thing in the morning. It's nothing personal, but in the end, I have nothing to say to you, and you have nothing to say to me.

The next morning, Mr. Saturday Night wants to fuck again, but I can't. I've got a headache and I want my apartment back. So I get up and make him coffee. So I tell him I have an appointment in an hour. So I offer him fresh towels, eucalyptus soap, and hair gel. I offer to refill his coffee. I find his socks tangled between the sheets, and even the empty condom wrapper. After his shower, I gallantly gather his coat, gloves, and scarf. I smile my brightest smile, and then we kiss the way strangers kiss: briefly, sweetly, and with no regret.

Intern

My vagina is not your soapbox. My vagina is not a place that you can claim to be sporting feminist values. My vagina is a talking mouth of petals, and it has something to say, and it goes something like this:

I'm looking for empowering and positive images of heterosexual sex. I'm coming out as a heterosexual woman.

I am a sexy twenty-something-year-old, and if I want to blow the president, I will, and if he wants to be blown, he will, and I thank God that the president of these United States is blow-able.

Because sister, sister, my vagina is not your soapbox. It is not a political orifice. It is a part of me, not separate. Don't further separate my sexuality from me in the name of sisterhood. I think fucking my boss is my prerogative. I think fucking our president should become a requirement of the White House internship program. In fact, I think knee pads should be issued to all subordinates in every office throughout America. Because I am the new young woman, and this is where I excel.

My vagina is not your soapbox. It is not yours. It is not "ours," there is no "we" women. And you are not my sister.

And as for myself, I wouldn't want your stanky slash as my soapbox. I'll step on your tackiness, I'll step right on top of your tacky bleach job and say: I know the intricacies of the president's prick, I know just how far down my throat he likes it to time with his shot into me. And you better believe I love the feeling of his spunk falling over my taste buds, running down my chin and down my throat. And that is why I've got the smile that all of America is seeing. Because my lips and teeth are sparkling with his anointment.

Addressing the Intern Situation

We worked together. She was my husband's secretary. I knew it the first day she walked in. I saw the look on his face, as if the answer to midlife crisis had just walked through the door. She wasn't at all pretty, but she looked at me out of the corner of her eye as if to say, "Those ten extra pounds on you might as well be seventy, because baby, I'm twenty-three years old, without a half ounce of extra body fat on me, and I rule the fucking world." Check.

She was trouble. Throwing fits, taking sick leave, coming in late and hung over. Every time she'd come in tardy with a document, he'd scold her. The disciplining of this young secretary gave him new life. No, it wasn't Viagra, it wasn't a forklift for the flaccid flower; it was "Tricia," the secretary.

I had just turned forty, and you know the rest of the story. He was fifty.

When he "confessed," I couldn't bring myself to sleep with anybody else for a year and a half. When Tricia entered my life, the girl inside me stood up and left my dying ovaries, walked into Tricia's body, as my life expectancy dropped in the blink of an eye. I was suddenly old. With her entrance, I was officially no longer the cutest and youngest girl in the room.

(She's on the couch in his office, in the same position in which I first made love to him, straddling him, he has yanked her pink panties to the side and entered her, her stick legs are coming out of the dress, and this time it's her sloppy mouth and her childish arrogant way, going, "Yes, yes, yes," and she's wearing those braids, and they're slapping her face back and forth as she says, "Oh, God, oh, God, oh, God!" And he smacks his mouth and then slaps her ass, "Yes!" And when he paws her dress off and it rips, it's not my breasts that fall out and fill his hands, it's her tiny tits that barely can be cupped in a hand, and he pulls really hard on her nipples. She writhes every time he twists them. She's a good actress. And her faking it is what's even more of a turn-on.

Another time—in the bathroom stall of the men's room, the ugly beige walls, the smell of piss—she's fingering herself, kind of spastic 'cause she's gangly like a colt, pulling up her little slip dress, almost keeling over on her wobbly high-heeled shoes as he's standing there, squished into this stall, with his tool in his hands, just his zipper open, saying, "Yeah, baby," and with the other hand he's stroking his balls, trying not to lose his spunk too fast, as she says "Oh, God! Oh, God, I'm coming!" Until her sloppy mouth opens up, and he beats off right into it.)

You may think rape fantasies are disgusting, but nothing compares to a year and a half of fantasizing to the loss of my childhood. The disgusting sight of this old man screwing this birdlike girl who had not a brain in her head. Yes, indeed, that which I know, that which I now understand—in my body—is arousing. The degrading, humiliating screwing of a little girl like in porno books, yes, was my fodder. My breath would quicken, and my voice would break, echoing alone in my room. And I would lie in my bed, broken, empty. What before had been my beautiful body was replaced by what I had bought—the magazine image of the starved twenty-three-year-old girl—the perfect woman of the twenty-first century. And she turned me on.

My finger still dipped inside me.

I remember being that girl, sleeping with married men. Yeah, I remember my flippant sideways stares, my disdain for feminism. Not understanding that I had the world by the balls because I was the fountain of youth. Every time I flipped my braids over my shoulders, every time a drop of sweat came off me, men would flock to drink it up. I had no idea. I thought I was just given this power and that it would last forever. Rose petals and flowers flowing from my lips.

I gave her my dying breath; it's in her, he entered her. I still have some of it left over, curled up in a ball. Sometimes I open it up, sit under her like a tree. And I wait for just one petal to fall and anoint me. Because inside me, I still think I'm that girl.

The Berlin Understudy

On her way to Berlin, she takes the tongue of a man at night between cars, he passes her chocolate and coffee, splashing onto her silk skirt, he takes her breasts in his hands like oranges, he peels the breasts, discards the rinds, dropping them to the floor of the train, she spies peasant's hands, stronger than any other, stubby fingers with dirt embedded in their lines, she longs to walk the lines of these hands, put her ear to the ground made of skin, listen to the song of his blood, the rivers and tributaries that beat toward his heart of hearts, and after the rinds that he has pulled off her navel-orange breasts have fallen to the floor, he eats the pieces—section by section—he takes the seeds in his mouth, slips them back into her mouth, she swallows the seeds, holds them down in the back of her throat, and all at once, after he has consumed her breasts, and the pulp sits, sticks to his teeth, the pale orange down his chin, they listen to the passing lights.

The train stops in Dusseldorf. She listens to a whistle, a sigh of closure, wheels of a cart come to sell them wine, she buys a bottle, warms her throat, and passes it to her stranger, who does not speak what she speaks, only looks at her with eyes that say, "You are the one, the one this moment." And later, in a hotel room with the light bulb swinging on a black cord that they hit with their feet, they laugh with red wine stains on their teeth and lips and make love in a bright fort made of white sheet—daytime going on outside—stories of purple vines rising up to their window for them, singing "Yes, yes, yes."

And after they do, he walks into the bathroom, washes himself, and goes out of view. She stares at the dripping faucet, the green toilet. He comes back to bed, and just as she decides to show him her frailty, that she is not just the tough sex pickup of the train, just as she shows him the tears in the corners of her mouth, just as she shows him that she is more than just a romantic quick screw in the night, that she is holding in her fingers her broken heart, held ridiculously together with the frail ribbon of hope, he abruptly says, "I must go."

"I must go to my wife." As if his accent has become stronger, as if he does not understand her language, as if he (does he?) needs a dictionary to interpret that she is a beating heart, human. The wetness down her cheek, no, not hysterical, no, not gonna hold onto you for dear life or swallow you whole, just not gonna be tough anymore...gonna fall in love. Not just a war story to tell the keys of her typewriter or her own future daughter..., but "...fall in love with me. Fall in love with me. And pretend."

"I must go, I must go, I must go to my wife," as he fingers his wallet and perhaps her picture, too. "It has been twenty-four hours, the train will be coming, I will say I was delayed for a day," he says, and she thinks, "Why not?" as she hallucinates his dropping money down. She turns to the glass stained with his lips on the side table. And he leaves.

She walks downstairs, past a pit bull marking his territory—back and forth—she smells flowers dripping down the front of their hotel. And then she smells piss, and the pit bull is going back and forth, pissing in this doorway and then pissing in a doorway three doors down—like Napoleon. He is marking his territory and she smells that it is a brothel, and he is the pimp. She sees a Parisian creperie and, in the midafternoon sun, she falls into it and sits at a long wooden table. She puts into her mouth fermented apple cider. Crepe. Sugar and lemon. It is late afternoon, they will close soon. Through the open window and screen door she sees the fruit flies come down the street. En masse. Their red eyes determined to find the fruit. As the lemon and sugar twist her mouth and she gulps into her cup. The cider. The men.

Marilyn Monroe

I am looking for a good fuck. A strong hard good fuck. A muscled man who will crush my lips. Crush them the same way wildflowers are crushed for perfume. That's what I want: a crushing, crushing kiss. Milk the sadness from my bones, baby. On a bed of dandelions, baby. On a bed of milkweed and gooseberries in the dry dirt of summer.

1950

He takes her dancing, this mother of three children, this still-married woman. He takes her dancing on a Saturday night in October, a blood moon in the sky. They drive into the big city. In the darkness inside the car, illuminated by the dashboard lights, he sees her silhouette, her face, the vegetable rise of her breasts, the small belly visible in her too-tight skirt, and knees as fine as carved ivory.

But more than this: this woman, this mother of three, still married but not to him, exudes an earthy, musky smell, as if he can still smell her womb opening in childbirth, the thick rush of blood, her hair and her arms drenched in sweat. He sees her naked—legs spread far apart—her breasts heaving with every contraction. He knows how open she is, how ripe and fertile, ready for anything. Ready for him.

Tonight he takes her dancing and holds her as close as he can. He puts his hand on the small of her back, he breathes into her hair, into her ear. She is helpless in his arms, he feels her heart quicken every time he touches her. But then she drinks too much. Her eyes become unfocused and her legs, once tight and confident, become slack. Her hair drips around her eyes. He takes her down to the lake. She falls into his arms, half-conscious. The blood moon unmasks and undresses this married woman, this mother of three, until she lays bare all her secrets:

Here is the tangled forest of pubic hair, here are the large brown nipples, larger and more luscious because three children have suckled here. Here are her moist lips, closed tight like a fist, like the first bloom of a scarlet rose, but they open wider and wider, to his hands, his tongue, and his mouth.

He wants to possess her, fill her with children. But she is too quiet. He sees that she is sleeping. He smiles, then drives her home. He took her dancing, this married woman, this mother of three children, he took her dancing, and now she belongs to him.

Mary Magdalene

Now, Nazareth is a hot little desert town and I am a young beautiful girl, ambitious and intelligent. And I need something in my life. I need truth. I need passion. I have a heart so big it hurts.

I hear about a man with dark eyes and a voice like raw honey. I hear he talks from the tops of mountains. I hear he preaches in a grove of olive trees, and the multitudes fall to their feet. I hear he's dangerous, and I know that I am already in love with him. I see him on Saturday. He stands in the river.

It is early morning and the light hits the water and enshrines his figure in gold. It is obvious, painfully obvious, that he is blessed, obvious that he is different. Jesus Christ is a holy man, yes. But he is also incredibly beautiful. And I don't care how he came into this life. I don't care who his mother is or who his father is—I just know that I have found what I have been looking for all my life. Love. I have found love. And by the way he looks at me, I know it is mutual. He walks up to me, and I don't know if it is a trick of the morning light, but he walks on the water. Not through it, but on it.

He asks if I am thirsty.

“If only you knew how thirsty I am. I could drink all the water in this river. I could open my mouth and swallow the whole of you and the river and still want more.”

He smiles. Takes my hand and leads me into the water. Kisses me. I feel his right hand on my breast, the other in the small of my back. Now it is late afternoon and the sky is pink and orange, and his hand moves up inside my robe and I am visited by a spirit so hot and so holy, I can’t stand up. I can’t breathe. I swear I can’t breathe.

“If only you knew how thirsty I am.”

He reaches up and unfastens his robe and it drops into the river. It floats alongside us, a piece of blue silk on the cool river. I kneel down and take the Son of God into my mouth. And he is sweet. I taste the tree of life, I bite into the apple, I suck the honey from the hive. I open my eyes and see twelve men watching us from the riverbank. I don’t like the look in their eyes. But he doesn’t seem to notice or care. He can’t stop kissing me. And when he does, he says my name:

“Mary Magdalene.”

Then he leads me into a grove of olive trees, pushes me up against a tree, parts my knees with his head of thick black hair so his tongue can enter me.

“Oh, God. Oh, God. Oh, God.”

I am so blessed. I am so in love. But it is a mistake to ignore the twelve men watching from the riverbank. I know somewhere deep in my soul that it is a mistake, but I can't stop. I watch miracles unfold before my eyes, yet every night he joins me in my bed. I see him between my legs, his long black hair fanned like feathers across my breasts. We are mortal. We are fallible. And we are in love. Except, one morning, I walk to the well for water and I hear:

"Whore."

An ugly word, utterly without grace or redemption. And I know it is the work of the Twelve Apostles.

"Whore"

reverberates every time I enter a room, drink a glass of wine, or stop for food. It's a small word uttered by small men. One morning, I am walking through the market and soon I am followed by an angry crowd. The hissing and whispering sound like a nest of vipers. I know what they want from me. They want me dead. I turn to face them—but he suddenly appears, picks up a stone, and says:

"Let anyone of you who is without sin cast the first stone."

I am not a whore and I have never been a whore, but it is too late. We escape to the hot Nazarene desert—we know we don't have much time; I can see it in his eyes. For forty days and forty nights we eat dried figs, drink red wine, and make love with a fury that sends the devil back down to hell. But when we return from the desert, everything has changed drastically. His best friend betrays him—and leads him into the hands of his enemies. He whispers in my ear:

"Where I am going, I am going alone."

And then he kisses me. The next time I see him, he is dragging a cross through a crowded street, and the blood drips like a scarlet river—he sees me and smiles. My love, the great love of my life, is crucified on a cross, his beautiful body twisted and bleeding. And his Twelve Apostles can do nothing to stop this.

It is no mistake that I see him first when he rises from the dead. It is no mistake. I see it in a dream—he walks into my room and tells me to wait at the tomb. He says to me:

"You gave me life everlasting."

I awaken the next morning while the sky is still gray. As he rises from the sepulchre, I know he is no longer human, but I am not afraid. His skin is cold as he places me on the rocks just as the sun begins to rise over his pale body. His skin is cold but his lips are warm. He whispers in my ear:

"Take me while I still have time."

I close my eyes and suck until the light of morning spreads through my limbs, until he sighs and screams and wakes up the birds in the olive grove. He rises from the rock of the sepulchre and walks west into town. I know I will pass into history as the whore in his life—but in truth I was his love, his lover, and his wife.

The Blue Hours

It rained a lot that first week up in the mountains, that first week in September. That's mostly what I remember, the rain and then his eyes in the rain, my arms around him, the sound of his breathing. He had trouble sleeping and I often found him in the early hours of the morning, a cup of coffee, cigarette glowing in the dark, watching the sunrise. "The blue hours," he called them. Love should've been enough to stop the blue hours from haunting him, but it wasn't. And I've never been known for my eloquence, but I would try. "Come back to bed," I would say, "come back to bed and let me keep you warm." But somehow his wife always intervened, even when she was two hundred miles away.

Our bed was impossibly damp. Large, graceful spiders, trapeze artists, swung over our heads, brown spots of mildew decorated the bedding, but of course I didn't care. I wore blue cotton pajamas and he would climb into bed at night and ask, "Why are you wearing pajamas?" And I would say, "So you can take them off." I closed my eyes as he undid the snap and slowly slid the pajama pants over my naked legs; then his mouth like a snail would slither back up my calves, my thighs, and into me. Then and only then would I open my eyes and look down at his thick head of hair, his large, muscular hands gripping my hips. I would sit up slightly and unbutton the top of the blue pajamas so that my breasts were exposed; I would grab them, squeeze them, rub my thumb around my nipples. Around and around.

When he came up for air, his face slick and wet from my cunt, I kissed him and loved the taste. Then his hands, soft and sure, pulled off the top of my pajamas until I lay naked in his arms, our hips softly grinding into each other, his voice whispering, whispering in my ear, "I love you. I love you." Love should've been enough, but it wasn't. Even as he slipped his cock easily, sweetly up inside me, even as I rose to meet his hips, sat up and wrapped my arms around his neck, riding him like a thoroughbred horse, elegant and sophisticated, and raked his back with my fingernails and called out his name, it wasn't enough.

In the morning, I always felt beautiful. Scrambling eggs and cutting up fruit, wearing a pink brassiere and his pajama bottoms loose on my hips, my belly button exposed, I would look down at my hands, glance at my reflection in the windows, the rain pouring down, and feel beautiful. On the thirteenth day, we packed up our suitcases and threw out the leftovers in the refrigerator, but instead of throwing out the flowers we had gathered on the mountainside, I wove them together to form a wreath and hung it from a nail on the front door. I knew we would not be back. We took separate buses back into the city, and when I got home my clothes were still damp from the rain in the mountains, and my eyes were damp, and the secret place inside me was damp, and I longed for his hands, his mouth, and his eyes, but love was not enough.

Mostly what I remember is the rain.

One Night in Moscow

Manhattan, 10:00 P.M., and the photographer packs up his equipment. He shows me the proofs, but I don't recognize myself because I am naked and beautiful. My entire body is geometry, sculpted by light, an exotic flower glances off my right shoulder, but I don't recognize myself. I can't help it and there's no use trying because I am very drunk and I have to go home. We started in on the champagne at seven, an entire magnum consumed mostly in the bathtub, covered in soap bubbles.

So I get dressed and leave the studio. I jump into a cab driven by a Russian émigré. He's twenty-two. When we get over the bridge, I start swearing at him because we're lost in Brooklyn and I'm drunk, so he pulls over and tells me I am an insensitive bitch. I apologize because he's right and invite him out to dinner. Because his family and my family are from Minsk. Because by now I am flat the fuck out of it.

I take him to dinner in my neighborhood. He orders a sandwich and several shots of vodka. I don't eat. I watch him, and I hear the plaintive strains of gypsy music, violins, and I see brightly colored scarves fluttering in the frosty morning air of Moscow. Then he asks me, "What else do you want to do?"

I say I want to drive to Coney Island in the rain, but instead we drive back into Manhattan. I am in the front seat of a yellow cab driving back over the Brooklyn Bridge, and my lover, my sweetheart, is the cabdriver. And for no particular reason, this makes perfect sense, it is the perfect romance. We are both from Minsk, immigrants, aliens, from a foreign country. He parks the car on First Avenue, we get out and go to another bar, have a drink. It is Saturday night and I am in rare form, gallivanting across two boroughs with an almost-child cabdriver. He is straining to act tough and impress the beautiful older woman he has somehow snagged. He lights cigarettes for me and places them in my mouth, he shows me the scars on his wrist. He fell in love and then she didn't love him, so he dragged a razor blade across his smooth young flesh. I tell him he is stupid, that I have done the same thing and that it's better to live. I can tell he's impressed. Suicide, it appears, is universal, cross-cultural…nobody can claim ownership of despair.

He searches the inside of my wrist for the scars and is disappointed when I tell him they are long gone. I order him a cosmopolitan at the bar. It's a red drink with a red cherry. It's pouring rain out and I'm also flirting with the bartender. I don't give a damn. I'm half out of my head. I'm drinking shitty white wine. I've been going at it now for hours, baby, for hours. He drives me home—my lover, my Russian émigré—and at my doorstep I kiss him long and deep, so long and so deep it's like oral sex. My tongue slides in and out of his mouth, like silk, like a snake. He is surprised to find me kissing him so deeply and so passionately. He is not prepared for this. He pulls back and searches my face for clues. I tell him:

"Darling, don't bother. I couldn't recognize her, either. I looked and I looked at those proofs and I saw nothing. And neither will you. Just let me kiss you so I can leave my imprint on your lips, so that on other nights like this you will dream about what it would be like to make love to a woman who cannot recognize herself, so you can learn how to lose yourself perfectly and passionately in the arms of strangers. And there is nothing more vulnerable than the inside of a young man's wrist."

But he doesn't listen to me. He can't. He's only twenty-two.

PART IV

Sex at Nineteen

Lola I: Mr. Natural

Last night, this guy at the bar offered me a hit of Mr. Natural. Mr. Natural is blotter acid. It's the size of a postage stamp, with a cartoon drawing of a fat man, and it's divided into four sections. If you take the entire hit, you get a free Quaalude. Well, I'm not that fucking stupid. That's what I said to him: "I'm not that fuckin' stupid. Keep your goddamn Quaalude." I've seen what happens to people who take the entire hit. Like Betsy. Betsy took the entire hit and ended up in some guy's bed in Chicago, for Christ's sake. She said, "There I am at four in the morning with come dripping down my legs and I ain't got ten bucks to take the train home."

The bar is really a nightclub called Tommy G's Circus. Tommy lives over the club in a maze of rooms decorated with black satin and psychedelic pictures. Piles of drugs everywhere. Famous rock bands play there every weekend.

Anyway, I'm at the club, I take a quarter of Mr. Natural, wash it down with bourbon and a couple of hits from a joint. The manager of one of the bands whispers in my ear, "I could make you scream." This immediately makes me wet. Make me scream? Nobody's made me scream. What have I got to lose?

I'm wearing a satin wrap dress. Upstairs in one of the dark bedrooms, he unwraps it, and underneath I am wearing only a pair of black panties. He yanks them down to my knees and pours peppermint schnapps onto my stomach. It drips down into my snatch.

He says, "It'll make it nice and sweet." Whatever. It just feels sticky to me.

All of a sudden I start getting off on the acid, but the bourbon and pot are making me sleepy. Next thing I know, I wake up and the drummer is going at me with his tongue. I sit up and say to him, "What the hell are you doing?" He's like, "You were lying there naked. Looking all luscious. I couldn't resist."

So I said to him, "Go fuck a duck." I wrap up my dress around my sticky hallucinating body and go into the living room, and my friend Betsy is running around naked. I can't believe the size of her tits. I think her nipples must be the size of dinner plates. The band is on break and they are taking turns sucking her tits and snorting coke.

Betsy makes me laugh, she really does. If I'm a dark green GTO on a set of mag wheels, Betsy is a white Corvette with a red-leather interior. If I'm a slut, she's a super slut. I just love her. She wears pants that are so tight her slit shows through. I run into John, the band's manager. I say, "What's with running out on me?"

He's like, "You passed out." I'm like, "You could've covered up my snatch." So I snort some coke to take the edge off the acid.

Then I'm back downstairs at the club, on the dance floor, dancing in my wrap dress minus my panties because I can't find them. Betsy is dancing with me and she's blissed out from having her titties sucked.

Later that night, she pulls a train; she's got the drummer in her mouth, sucking on his doglike cock, and the lead singer is fucking her in the ass, and the manager is eating her pussy. And Tommy G, Master of Ceremonies, is just laughing away.

When I'm not fingering myself, I am wiping the come and peppermint schnapps from my body.

I am nineteen years old and I am wearing cherry lip gloss.

Adam

I scraped the heroin addict off the street with the gentle sliver of my right toe, the snow caught my clit, and I smelled night before the first day of school, January 8, 1983. A snowstorm, and the hair covered his eyes, falling like a feather boa, his eyes popped up at me, not so much like a cartoon, which he indeed was, but like the sexy sleepy look of Al Pacino in *The Godfather*. He giggled and asked if I'd like to get a drink, and we fell into the misty western Massachusetts sushi bar–slash–nightclub–slash–hot tub joint, and before I could finish my last drink he commented on my cowboy boots and I asked, "Do you want to come see the rest?" We stood above the lined-up boots—aqua and red and brown—in my Smith College dorm room. The heroin addict turned to me and said he'd like to get inside my shoes and I took this as a come-on as I fell back onto the futon, quite a ride down, and reached my hand over to the ghetto blaster to hit Springsteen's *Nebraska*. He dialed the phone to call his girlfriend who lived in a nearby town. He told her he "wouldn't be coming home," as he ran his hand up my leg and I put my hand to his corduroy jeans and his hard nineteen-year-old heroin-addicted cock. He talked practically the entire time, and smoked while he fucked me, his mouth going a mile a minute, so much that we never even kissed. I was below him—the soil—he was on top of me, chattering away, a shot of whiskey, arousal, and nicotine climbing up to his face. He was a dictator, Napoleon, Lenny Bruce, Sly Stallone, his tool drilling me and spinning as he sliced me into bits that night—and in a weird way I liked it—but I knew that he was really a carcass. The exoskeleton of some young man who was trying to fill himself up as I laid myself at his feet—my soiled openness as a succor, a savior, or an angel—on a trip to be seeded, as he sprayed himself across my face to know he was there.

Lola II: Lola and Betsy

I sell crystal meth on the side. Not because I need the money. I live at home, for Christ's sake. I sell drugs because it's cool to sell drugs. I don't even know what crystal meth is. I know it burns the shit out of my nose when I snort it. I guess I get high from it, but I prefer cocaine.

One night I snort so much of something, I pass out on the dance floor. My friends let me sleep until I wake up and start dancing again. Then Black Dog, who drinks there every night, says he needs to fuck me. Now he is a skinny crazy-assed little bastard who makes me laugh, but I never saw myself fucking him. Then Clint, the bartender, says, "Let's go upstairs and have ourselves a group fuck."

But before that happens, Black Dog passes out on the bar stool. So it's just me, Betsy, and Clint. Clint, who is fat and married and also Tommy G's best friend.

Listen, I just love what Betsy is wearing: a red polyester tube top over her size-38 double-D tits and skintight white pants. Her black curly hair is fluffed up into a 'fro and her lips are Dark Berry, from her mom's Avon collection. When Clint pulls his pants off, his prick is tiny, about the size of my pinkie.

Betsy and I look at each other and smirk: You're gonna fuck us with that?

Whatever. Clint stands there yanking at it to make it bigger. We get naked and get on the bed. I put one of Betsy's tits in my mouth, just to see what all the fuss is about. Clint is stroking my ass and Patsie's tits feel like the pillows over at my grandma's house. I don't have tits. I am flat-chested and long-waisted, but I do have a nice ass.

At one point, Clint does the Don Juan routine. He lies back and strokes both of us, but we're not fooled. This fat married guy can't get it up. At this point I am bored and desperate to smoke a cigarette. I got a math test tomorrow and I can't spend all night working on this guy's cock. Suddenly he jumps on top of me with his little prick in his hands, and he tries to stick it in me.

Betsy gets jealous because she's in love with him. So she jumps off the bed, and goes into the next room, leaving me with Mr. Little Prick, and I'm thinking, thanks! Thanks a lot!

So I'm oohing and aahing. So I'm moaning and groaning. While he pretends to fuck me, I'm watching Betsy cry on the couch. I shoulda went upstairs with Black Dog. The size of his cock is legendary.

Clint finally shoots his wad inside me and I think, thank God.

I leave him on the bed and walk over to Betsy. She's not mad at me. I say, "Look, if you're so hot for the guy, go back in there. As for me, baby, I am outta here."

So much for romance. I don't even wait to put my clothes on. I walk naked down the stairs and into the bar. What the fuck. It's Tuesday and it's only Tommy G behind the bar and Black Dog passed out on the bar stool.

Body Builder

It was the body builder named Bart who could get an erection again the second after he came, and whose abs and pecs felt like the tits of a woman, but they were hard, and his ass was like a rock, his body constantly shaved. I played Puck and he was Bottom and it was after a show—I was in the shower, backstage, a private stall—when, Bottom, who had flirted with me during the mechanicals scene for a whole month, appeared. His donkey ears off, an erection. He came up behind me and in a South Boston accent told me to put my hands behind my back, which I did, and I grabbed his smooth, twenty-year-old, steroid-endowed prick and brought it up to what I now recall was my own perfectly smooth bottom, just skin and bones, and little titties that pressed into the tile as he pulled his cock and smeared it up and down my cheeks until I felt his hot spunk hitting my upper back. The jism flew because of his youth, and he remained erect. He said, "Suck me." A minute later, "Put your fingers in your pussy." A second later, "Ride my cock," which I did as he lay back in the shower and I finally placed him inside of me. He ordered me to put my pussy-drenched fingers into my mouth, which I did. And then into his mouth, which I did. And then back into my mouth. I left my finger dangling on my lower lip, arched my back like a six-year-old, and came. I would ride home with this man Bart on his motorcycle, back to his U. Mass apartment, to get screwed yet again in his waterbed. The next day he shaved his legs before driving me back to Smith College, where I dismounted his slumming cock and fell into my anti-phallic theory class.

Threesome

I was seventeen. On the East Coast looking at colleges, and he was with me because it was Passover and his grandparents lived in Paramus. So while I went up to Smith, he sat on their La-Z-Boy and waited until I came down from the snowstorm to see him in a yarmulke and taste Manischewitz.

It happened on the Saturday that we took the bus into Manhattan to meet Clay, who worked in films and had a loft in the Bowery. My boyfriend and Clay had been best friends from the time that they were in boarding school together. And even before that, when they lived on the commune. Two kids who had been encouraged, yes, to smoke pot at the age of eight, who grew up naked together. It was intriguing to me—their past—and what would become of their future.

When I met Clay, I saw that he had pockmarked skin and I loved his face immediately. I wanted to kiss his skin, his green eyes. He had cocaine and we went to see *Quest for Fire*, and we laughed and laughed and called it *Quest for Babe*. And then we drank bottles of champagne in his loft with no walls. We sat down at his roommate's vanity, and I asked the two boys to put on makeup, which they did.

They were nineteen.

My boyfriend asked me to take off my underwear from beneath my skirt, and I did. Then Clay opened a drawer and pulled out white stockings and garter belts, and I said they should put them on, and they did. I went to the gravity boots and laced them, and my boyfriend lifted me up. He hooked me upside down and my skirt flew over my face, but I didn't care, and my boyfriend brushed his fingers over my triangle of hair while Clay turned his back. And the next moment we were having political arguments at the table. I was sitting at the head, and as we were talking. Clay put his hand under the table and slid it between my legs. I didn't let my boyfriend know what was happening; I just let Clay stroke me and made funny eyes at him as we tried to keep the consistency of our sentences and he gently touched my clitoris. Until I simply asked my boyfriend if it was OK, and before he could answer, I leaned over—with Clay's fingers now inside me—and kissed my boyfriend, and he liked it. And then I kissed Clay.

Then we're on the bed and all my clothes are off and there's a flash where the two of them kiss each other and then they smirk and giggle and turn back to me, but then my boyfriend enters me from on top, and while he's screwing me Clay kisses me. But then I can't stop myself: I pull Clay's body up so I can take him in my mouth.

I am seventeen.

I know that inside my boyfriend is scared to be doing this. But when he comes, Clay gets on top of me right away, and I say, "No babies and no disease," and I ask him not to come in me, and I ask him if he has herpes. I feel obligated. It is 1981. And then he starts to screw me and we're getting into it, and I like my boyfriend's best friend. A lot. But then my boyfriend starts beating on Clay's back with his fist, and when we look, my boyfriend is crying in a ball at the end of the bed and the sun is coming up, and I see that there are gargoyles outside the window, and I feel like vomiting. I lie back and sleep for half an hour and we leave an hour later for Port Authority to take the bus to Paramus. We walk down the empty, early-morning Bowery streets. We are husks. Not so much from the sex as from the drugs and alcohol. But also from the betrayal. And we realize that we may be the kids of hippies, but we still know possession and love. We wonder if we'll ever get over it. Because we love each other. And we hold each other and apologize. But we are bombed out. Our skin now smelling like Clay's. I was seventeen.

Trina the Trickster

Trina is a twat. A trickster. When everybody is high from three bowls of hashish, she sneaks a pack of exploding matches into the festivities. She watches her friends' faces light up when they smoke another bowl with the trick matches. She laughs explosively. Nothing could be funnier. They get back at her: they sneak the same matches into her bag. Late at night, she is home alone, very drunk. Sitting on the toilet, lighting a cigarette. Bam! She laughs again and again. Pulls out the vibrator from under the bathroom sink, flips the switch, smiles her way through orgasm after orgasm, and watches the sun come up as she comes.

Trina is a twat. A beauty. Seventeen years old. A straight-A student on the honor roll, she can suck cock like nobody's business. She smokes pot from a brass cock, the balls are the bowl...no boy on earth will smoke dope from that pipe. What does she care? She knows she sucks cock like nobody's business. She knows how to tickle the underside of the erect shaft with the tip of her pink tongue. Then she rolls the smooth head in her mouth like a piece of candy until one pearly drop of come drips off the tip. Goes in for the kill, slides the prick deep inside her mouth, grabs the base with her hand, and squeezes the balls. Loves it when they squirm and moan.

Trina is a trickster, a twat, and her tits are small and hard. Gets straight As and poses provocatively for her English teacher. He's so hot for her he can barely dangle his participles. He's so hot for her long legs and her tight tits, he doesn't give her detention when she whips rubber bands at the dumb kids in her class. He looks the other way. He looks at her. Trina loves spitballs, rubber bands, English literature, and sucking cock.

Immature

I got it in England from the chemist. You piss on a stick every morning and it reads your hormone level, tells you if you can make love that day. It's made for more "mature couples" who don't mind if they do get pregnant. I piss on the stick like you piss on my hand. We do this as a pastime one night in front of the fire. "Put your hand out," and I do, and you piss all over it. You open another bottle of wine and I don't wash my hand, we leave it on the stone floor, it doesn't smell at all, we set off a spinning firecracker on top of it, and I don't mind the 6 percent chance of getting pregnant, do you? Because we are so mature.

Lola III: Lola on Stage

I celebrate my seventeenth birthday at Tommy G's Circus by singing on stage with a famous rock-and-roll band. I am coked up and dressed to kill: silver lamé halter top over my tiny cherry nipples, long denim skirt, and silver platform shoes. The lead singer smiles at me; I smile back and take him upstairs.

He's got long blonde hair, a skinny ass, and he's wearing a pair of women's pantyhose with nothing underneath, a sequined topcoat, and orange suede boots. He's young, younger than me, and really shy for a rock-and-roll star, so I gotta do all the work once we get upstairs. First, I pull off his orange suede boots and unwind the pantyhose down around his knobby knees, and his prick is really cute and stands straight up when I wrap my mouth around it. It tastes like a pickle. It looks like a pickle, too.

He's got only twenty minutes before he's got to be back on stage, so I line up some coke on the table, and while he bends over to snort it, I stick the pickle back in my mouth. He starts giggling and I start giggling and then it's like I've got a golden retriever following me around the room begging me to put his cock back into my mouth. I've taken off my denim skirt but I keep on my platform shoes, my panties, and my halter top. But when I bend over to light a cigarette, he pulls my panties down and sticks his pickle in my ass and I start screaming!

I've never been fucked in the ass before, and it's painful. I'm like, "You know I won't be able to sit down for a week." And he's breathing really hard and saying, "Easy, easy, baby." But there's nothing easy about being fucked in the ass! Wait till Betsy hears! She told me that Clint rammed it up inside her ass last week. And what she's doing fucking that fat married guy, I will never know.

But now I'm a little more relaxed, now I feel myself opening up to him, and he feels it, feels my ass opening up, softening up, and he says, "Give it up, baby, give it to me," so I arch my back and his pickle slides in even deeper and he's got both hands on my tits and I'm holding onto the edge of the couch for dear life. I'm terrified I'll tip over in my platform heels.

It's hard as shit keeping my balance and my legs start shaking and I'm even starting to sweat, but now it's like his cock has been up inside my ass forever and a day, and it's sweet, oh, God, it's so sweet.

I'm Sister Slut and I'm being fucked up the ass by a rock-and-roll star and it's my birthday and I've still got half a gram of coke.... It feels like he's going to come, so I pull his prick out of my ass and shove it deep inside my throat because now I'm coming and he's coming and it's like happy birthday to you, baby!

Back downstairs, he sings "Rebel Rebel" by David Bowie because he knows it's my favorite song, so I lean up against the stage singing along because I know all the words and he pulls me up to him and gives me the mic. I can't believe it! I am the envy of every girl in Tommy G's Circus.

I'm singing on stage wearing the hottest pair of shoes in the world and I got the hottest rock-and-roll singer by the balls.

Karamu

Briefly, they were lips like cushions, and white teeth. As my African dance teacher finished the joint with me outside the dance studio in Amherst, he leaned into me on his cane and kissed me like honey, like heaven. A kiss I will never forget, no hips, just light like a bird, like a feather. And then I went back to my dorm, missed dinner, but made it to my dishwashing job to slam shut the industrial washer—high as a kite—as the other pearled, monogrammed, sweatered Smithies stacked dishes and sorted silverware, and I thought about how I had just kissed my teacher.

Two Girls

She had slits of blue eyes, and cigarettes popping in and out of her mouth. Like cherry coke around her lips, she looked like she had just sipped something and not wiped her mouth—very red lips that were thin and a little cruel. Black mascara and blonde hair like feathers just above her scalp. She was a punk rocker from East Cambridge, with the voice of Jodie Foster, black-leather leg warmers, and a camera that she held onto for dear life—nighttime flash photography of dismal places. I had met her in my Advanced Nude Photography Seminar. She showed me pictures of burned-down houses and I imagined making love to her inside them. She showed me altars to her boyfriend and I imagined knocking them down. Her room was like the child's room I had always wanted. I convinced her to get into my dorm by telling her to go cry to the dean, and the next thing I knew she not only lived with me and one hundred other women, but she was my best friend, and we smoked on her single bed as the snow fell on my birthday, and she took me out into the cold, gave me a rocking horse and a bottle of champagne, and thoroughly made me fall in love with her as we passed by the swing that Martha swung on in the movie version of *Who's Afraid of Virginia Woolf*.

It was not until after we graduated that one night we found ourselves in an eighties hot tub, all by ourselves, after all the loser older townies had left, and she asked if she could kiss me—oh, God—and she leapt across the water at me and took my face in her hands, and for the first time I felt a woman kissing me—and George Winston was playing—and I smelled cedar and chemicals or whatever hot tubs are made of, and she was climbing all over me, slipping across my white body with her tiny nipples, and she told me how beautiful I was. And later, inside the shower, she looked at me like the end of the world and I closed my eyes and imagined the burned-out house she would make love to me in, and how I would not run away from this promised life, love of women and every single fucking thing that goes along with it, but I would stay with the dyke in me, embrace the fucking Amazon, and I would run away with her forever, this girl I had fallen in love with the second I caught a glimpse of her slit blue eyes. But I didn't. I turned away. I never inserted even a finger inside another woman or really even inside myself. I'd say, "I don't do that with women, go below the belt, the taste: no." So I went through my twenties with semen shot down my throat and I swallowed every time, wondering about everything I had missed the moment Elena plunged her fingers inside me—my best friend—and I started to cry and I said, "No," as I grabbed my clothes and ran from the room. In 1985. At Smith College.

PART V

Wet Dreams

When He Kisses Me

In my dream, he pulls the sheets back and they are clean, a clean, white-silk landscape. He stands over me and takes off his clothes, lies down next to me, pours me a glass of cold champagne. Pours the champagne over my naked body, licks it up, and makes love to me. Afterward, I am wrapped up in his white robe. He thinks I am unattainable, fashionable, and passionate. I sit silently, inscrutably, and lap up my hot coffee. It will take him a lifetime to get inside my head, inside my heart, but he is willing to wait. Because, by God, here is a woman worth waiting for.... He doesn't say this with words, but I can tell it is what he is thinking. I can tell because when he kisses me, his tongue lingers over every curve and muscle inside my mouth.

If I...

OK, I want a huge dick and I want to suck it. I want an enormous prick and I want to masturbate all day long. I want to pull it out and show it off. I want to suck it, suck it, and then suck it again. I want to walk down Christopher Street—past the cigar store on Sheridan Square—and have men look at the bulge in my pants. I want them to pull me into a nearby alleyway and masturbate with me. I want to wipe off my come with an old sock, I want to be able to get it up again right away, and have the tip covered in white jism. I want to fuck a girl really hard and watch her come, and then I want to go eat a ham and pastrami sandwich with mustard, and then I want to throw her over and fuck her again really really really hard from behind, watching us in the mirror. Then I want to stroke my big big big balls. And when I come, I want to pull out of her twat and spray it on her lips. And then I want to walk away with my huge schlong, thinking I'm so fucking great.

Movie Star

Dressed in red silk, you are at a dinner party and for some reason you forgo your usual cocktail of Nembutal and champagne. The large house sits next to the ocean. You are petted and photographed, fawned over. Every man in the room wants you to sit on his face.

Your dress is skin-tight and you are not wearing underwear. Your ass and your tits undulate like water balloons and you are the most beautiful woman in the room, but it means nothing to you.

Desiring a breath of fresh air, you step out onto the patio and hear voices coming from the sea.

Immediately you know: sirens. Singing to you for one night and one night only.

So without a backward glance, you kick off your jeweled stilettos, and as you enter the water, the sea slides open and insinuates itself into you, slowly, deliciously, the way you always dreamed it would. The water reaches up and penetrates your mouth, your ears, while the song of the sirens grows louder and sweeter. Your breasts are caressed and kissed. You linger in the surf, buoyant, ecstatic, until the ocean rocks you to orgasm.

Scotland

I walk up a hill that is covered in peat moss. Pregnant bunnies scurry away; two scared bucks run past me. I get to the mansion and it is now dark. The door is made of heavy wood and metal; a strong lead ring turns to let me into the castle. I walk in and am struck by the fact that nobody is there. The wind whistles and pounds like it has its own personality through the chimneys of the hundreds of fireplaces and against the old smeared leaded windows of Ballencrieff.

I walk up to the brocade—very intricate—that covers the walls, and I see that it is lined in clefts. Slightly wet, glistening, delicate little jewel boxes. When I stick my finger into one, it sucks my finger lightly, like a mouth. Then I put all my fingers inside, and finally press my entire fist inside this pudendum. From the winding staircase beyond the doorway, a flock of disembodied snatches breeze through the air and into the room. One comes up to my mouth and kisses me. As I gently fist the velvety purse on the wall, this other twat necks with me, its clitoris running along my teeth, and I put my tongue deep into this soft soft vulva. While it undulates, the walls moan, and the trees outside sing.

The kissing cunt lightly grazes my face and moves through the air, pulling me into another room that is lined in breastwork. It brings me over to one of the most beautiful ivory orbs. I step right up and take its nipple in my mouth, and the walls groan again, the wind outside is rushing now, one of the windows bursts open and the wind lifts up my shirt. My nipples are grazed by what feels like spirits from the Pictish caves beneath Ballencrieff.

And then, on the floor below me, I see more knobs, but these are pointed and hard, and although they are breasts, they are also peckers. I sit on a pecker/nipple, put it deep inside me, and twist as I continue to suck the rack on the wall. A host of gashes start to rip off the rest of my clothes and suckle around my cleavage. Milk shoots out of the breast that I'm worrying with my tongue, and my nipples are bitten by the tiny disembodied muffs as I twist harder and harder on the breast/phallus with my pudendum. It's starting to come and I clench down on it, pull away to watch it spurt out and fly through the air, all the way to the ceiling, where angels are painted in clouds. I lie back and the nether lips gather to my pussy and finish me off. I come in a slow-motion ecstasy, my hips straining and pressing up into the air, my fingers clutching the floorboards.

The aristocrat of the house comes in from her room, where she's done her toilet, and she tells me that I have broken the rules of the house. She asks, "...Don't you know that the tea and biscuit tray is to be brought up the narrow winding stairway every day at four, that dinner is served at seven, sherry no later than six-thirty, and after-dinner tea at eight? What are you doing?"

"Sorry, ma'am," I say, and put my apron on over my steaming gusset and hallucinate no more that I am the woman of the house, but know that I am again the cook, come to bake the pastries and pour the tea at Ballencrieff.

Subway Fantasia

It's July, and the subway is hot. A packed tin of pickled fish, a slow-moving ocean of hot bodies. The train moves and rocks up against the slow press of arms and limbs and my hand strains to catch the strap over my head. My pink silk blouse has come unbuttoned; one dark nipple peeps over the top. Oh, no! The businessman in the expensive silk suit sweats and grins. He can see me. But I don't move. I don't move to button my blouse or adjust the strap—I let him look and I get hot. Our eyes meet but now we don't smile. We will never know each other. But right now we are lovers, anonymous lovers in the hot press of rocking bodies in late July.

"That's right, lover. Come here, lover. Run your tongue over the rough silk of my breasts. You can only use your mouth; your hands can't touch me or possess me. Open your mouth; you are wordless and shirtless."

When the train stops, I reluctantly lower my arm. The heat outside the station assaults my limbs, my legs are weak. I can hardly walk. Deep inside my apartment, I turn up the air conditioner and hang black silk from every window. I peel off my clothes until I am naked. Then I prop a mirror in the living room, and I dress up in fishnets and an amber-colored mink. I slip on spike heels. Slow-moving jazz on the stereo and lips stained dark red. I become a dancer in a dark room of men who want me so badly they would die for me, but they can't touch me. They can look, but they can't touch. Suddenly I am Cleopatra, slow dancing on the Nile. My eyes are rimmed with kohl and my pussy is smudged pink and red. The champagne is pink and goes to my head. I bend over and run my hand up the length of my leg, a hush falls over the room.

The fat man in the corner gasps—he can't take it—his heart stops. I think he might be dead. Suddenly, the doorbell rings—it is the dimwitted plumber from next door. He enters the room and takes a seat to my left. He unzips his pants while I lie on the glass-topped coffee table and spread my legs. His tongue enters me and a storm of silver and gold coins rain down around me. I have started a riot of hot men who want me but can't touch me. The sharp point of my heel enters the plumber's mouth. He licks the black leather—he doesn't know I am the hot blonde from next door. He rips off my mink. I am completely naked, charged up and ready to rocket into the universe. An alabaster goddess from another time. A hot whore with nothing on her mind.

When it is over, I hang the mink in the closet while applause rings through the vacant room. It is summer again, and the windows are empty and cool.

The Mirror in the German Hotel

She's lying across his lap with her blushing cheeks in the air, her skirt hiked up, her panties around her ankles, and she's wearing Mary Janes—though she is twenty-five years old.

She is his assistant, and he is the theater director.

He is looking straight ahead at the mirror in this German hotel room, while she is on the verge of aroused tears. And he is counting—very slowly, from one to one hundred—his hand raised above her ass that is waiting, waiting, waiting, for the hand to come down upon its soft curves.

But it doesn't.

He just sits—stone-faced and cruel—looking at himself in the mirror. When he gets to ninety-four, he tells her to stand up, go to the corner, and face away from him. He orders room service. She stays there even when the waiter comes up, and the waiter blushes and grabs the tip and leaves.

On the elevator, the waiter stares at the numbers as he goes down to the basement—ten, nine, eight, and it's moving ever so slowly—seven, six, five—but he cannot get his prick to stop going up, and—to his sadness—he has got a fat prick, and it is always impossible to hide. The elevator stops on three, and a woman in a fur coat steps in. She is thirty-nine years old and has been crying. She raises her hand to her neck, touches her collarbone, and adjusts the thin necklace that traces a line around her throat, almost in slow motion, while he watches. And then his eyes go to her eyes, which are directed toward his crotch. He blushes and she hits the emergency stop. She asks the waiter to recite a children's rhyme in German.

She unzips his trousers and delicately removes what is now a fully filled and erect prick. She goes to her knees and begins her duty as he strains to look down her fur coat at her gigantic ivory cleavage. And when he almost comes, she suddenly releases him and deactivates the emergency stop so that the doors fly open. He whimpers like a small child and quickly closes his fly.

Another boy is revealed, standing with a full platter of food. He enters with a swish, the elevator doors shut, and the new boy inadvertently looks down at the slightly wet crotch of the blown waiter's trousers. He smiles and looks straight at the waiter because now he's got a boner, too.

When the elevator gets to the first floor, the woman exits. She enters the phone booth and dials. A woman answers and asks, "Do you want a blow job?" The woman in the phone booth spreads her legs slightly and grinds a black pump into the floor. She replies, "Yes," as she notices—through the window of the phone booth—that the twenty-five-year-old assistant to the theater director is racing out of the hotel doors and into a cab.

The girl is in tears, and after she gets in the cab, she climbs from the back seat into the front seat, lifts her skirt, pulls her panties down to her ankles, and places herself down on the rounded head of the stick shift. The cabby is horrified, and his eyes pop out of his skull as she rides the stick shift. The car lurches forward and she begins to sing as she fucks the taxi and the cabby attempts to keep the car driving properly.

She now pulls up her shirt and twists her almost completely flat nipples and continues to sing and be naughty, until the car stops shifting and glides along. She puts her head back and is quiet for several moments—climaxing. The cabby stares at her, his mouth wide open, as the taxi crashes right into a tree. A branch breaks through the side window and several crimson apples fall around them. The cabby—who now has a bloody cut in his forehead—takes a bite of an apple as he looks down at what is now the theater director's dead assistant. He pulls her panties from around her Mary Janes.

He gets out of the taxi and goes to the edge of the road. Sirens approach and he buries her panties in the earth. The paramedic tends to the cut on his forehead as the theater director's dead assistant is put on a stretcher and a sheet is pulled up and over her eyes. The paramedic looks into the cabby's eyes with a small flashlight and immediately puts him into the ambulance.

It takes off with a wail, leaving a group of onlookers and one little girl, who has watched the whole scene. The little girl toes the soil and pulls out—between her big toe and the next toe—the pair of white ruffled panties. She holds them up and then slowly and meticulously lifts her leg very high into the air until she deliberately places it over her shoulder, and the foot bearing the panties emerges around the other side of her neck. And what is revealed, of course, is her snatch.

The crowd gathered around the scene of the accident watches, and several women with large breasts leave in disgust. Several men pull their pricks out and start to beat off as the girl standing on one leg spins around and bounces. She hops into the forest, and one of the men from the crowd follows her. When he gets into the forest, he cannot find her in the brush.

She suddenly appears, hanging upside down on two legs from a branch, the panties now in her teeth, and she slaps him and he falls to the ground. She swings around and around the branch like a trapeze artist and does a flip through the air and runs away through the woods. The man stands up, wipes the dirt from his pants, and brings his hand to his cheek, inadvertently leaving dirt on his skin. He runs through the pines after the girl. He comes to a small wooden house and there is smoke coming out of the chimney and it smells like bacon. He opens the door to find the girl being fucked by a wolf that is wearing a bonnet. The wolf keeps hammering at this girl and then she rolls off its prick and vanishes into thin air. The man looks at himself in the mirror above the bed, and the wolf howls and jumps out the window.

The man looks down from the mirror and he is back in the German hotel room with his assistant's bottom in his lap. She is crying and he is at number ninety-four. And then he says, a bit louder, sternly, and almost sadly:

Ninety-five.

Ninety-six.

Ninety-seven.

Ninety-eight.

Ninety-nine.

One hundred. And the hand comes down.

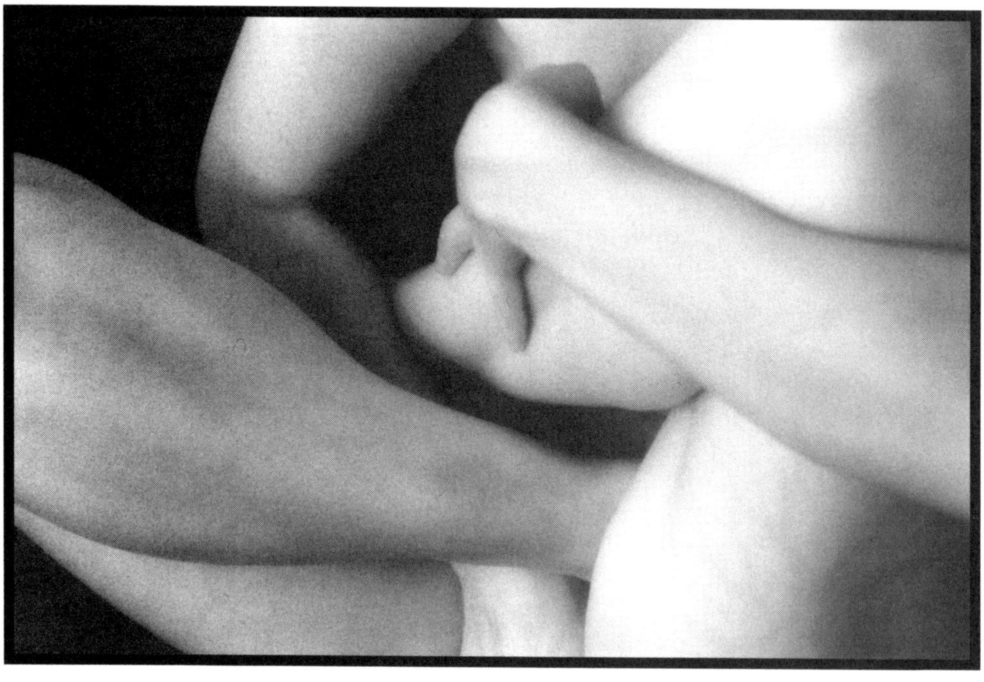

PART VI

Don't Move

Cock in Your Mouth

"I'd love to see you with a cock in your mouth" is how it started. Out of the blue, the conversation had been perfectly normal up until then, on the phone, across the country. Perfectly civil up until that moment, and then it all changed.

Lap Dance

Elana leans out of the garden of evil with all the sinuous beauty of a snake. She girds my lap with warm breath, her breasts are loose beauties swinging, swinging, she is a young Cleopatra with dark eyes, and when I look deep into them, I hear the sound of rain. She whispers in my ear, "What do you do?" And I say, "I am a writer." And then I want to ask—but I don't—"Elana, when you dance naked in a room filled with rich young men, who has the power? You and your sisters, with your long lean bodies, your smooth faces and your soft breasts? And how do you live in your body when it is not dancing for men?"

She swirls and she dips and she sways. I have a large smile on my face as she puts her knees between my legs so she can dance closer to me. I smile because it is intoxicating to have such beauty before me. As she turns her back and elevates her perfect ass, I want to ask her again, "Elana, darling...who has the power? It's important that you tell me. It's important that you tell me that you have the power. As you slip out of your sequined evening gown, as it slides over your alabaster shoulders, as your breasts spill out into the smoky air, as your smile widens with every gyration of your hips, it's important that you have the power. And when you go home, when you wash off your makeup, when you relinquish your Cleopatra wig, when you are just a girl in front of the mirror, how do you get your body back?"

Don't Move

He said, "Don't move," and I'd squirm and make a noise and he'd say, "Don't move," his pants were half off, and I was stroking his bulging cock. I was between his legs, facing away from him, fully dressed, except my panties were down at my ankles, and with one hand he was stroking my clit and with the other he was fucking me with one finger in my cunt and another in my ass—and with his hot breath, he was in my ear, too. He just kept saying, "Don't move, don't move, don't move, don't move," until he stroked my clitoris to hallucination. I turned around and strapped myself onto him, shoved his big horse cock into my cunt and fucked him really hard. He threw me over, put his hand to my neck—really tight—and said, "Don't move, don't move," as he slid in and out of me really slowly until he came. Afterward, he put his fingers back inside me, got hard again, and fucked my mouth with his prick at the same time that I masturbated and came. He shot his wad down my throat. He turned on some porno and started to piss on me, I spread my legs and then stuck his cock right in me, and he fucked me again, saying that I was a "good little fuck," that that felt "really good," his "prick going into your wet cunt." And then he turned me over and shoved himself into me violently and I screamed, and he said, "I like that," and he grabbed my hair like reins and fucked me as we watched in the mirror. His shirt came off and I looked at his tits, which were bigger than most women's—hard and gorgeous. He came into my hair and down my neck, and then I stood up and fingered myself as he watched. Finally, at four in the morning, we fell asleep, covered in come.

Black Jacket

I hook my hands into the pockets of my new black jacket. I stop for a glass of wine at a local bar and the Spaniard to my left is licking my face with his deep dark eyes. I sit back and let him admire the geography of my neck and the swell of my breasts. Three hours later, he is feeling me up in my garden. I am on his lap, facing him, and he is furiously trying to unzip my pants. I say, "It's late, it's late," but he doesn't care. I tell him to leave but he doesn't care. He says, "I won't leave until you show me your tits." I tell him no. I turn around, and he unhooks my bra. Now I am afraid.

Rape, 1955

She's in this student's car trying to unlock the door, and her hand is shaking. The mascara, carefully put on to look pretty for the night class that she teaches at the state university, is raining down both cheeks. She proudly teaches English as a second language, with her recent Stanford Ph.D. and her narrow escape from the Kentucky mountains. Her lipstick, now faded to pink, is smeared across her cheeks and surrounds her mouth.

He's sitting back, this Iranian student, the knife still in his hands.

As she fumbles for the door, she's also going for her keys, trying to get them between her fingers; she's gonna gouge his eyes out.

She analyzes what she's done to provoke this as she pushes her legs against him and bites his cheek. This only turns him on more as he rips the sleeve off her below-the-shoulders ruffled blouse and sees the bra, lacy and pointy, typically fifties.

She thinks, Good thing I never pierced my ears, as he rips her earrings off, expecting blood, but there is none. He throws the turquoise earrings into the back seat and pulls his cock out. But he's not hard for some fucking reason and he starts playing with himself with one hand, holding her neck down with the other.

(She sees herself teaching, in her platform shoes, her lipstick, her blonde hair, her flirtatious way. And how she has to wear sweat guards pinned under her arms because teaching is so invigorating.

When she turns her back on the class and writes something on the board, is that when he envisions giving her a ride home and detouring up to Twin Peaks to rape her?)

She's laughing to herself, and a little bit out loud. "Not much of a rape without an erection." And she socks him in the face.

"Shit!" he yells, and she socks him in the stomach. This floors him, and he sits back, half-laughing and almost satisfied as if he really did fuck her.

"But he didn't," she keeps saying to herself over and over again as she runs down the hill, trying to find a residential neighborhood where she can go to a house and call the police or a cab.

Pretty soon she's holding the platform shoes in her hands and walking in her stocking feet. She's afraid she looks like an Italian whore.

And sure enough, the policeman doesn't believe her story when she leans into his car. But he drives her home anyway. She sits in the back seat, behind the metal grating, watching the lights of San Francisco pass, flickering by her, those lights that told her ten years ago that she had made it, and that the horrors of the Kentucky mountains were way behind her now.

Holiday in Brazil

One hot, very hot afternoon in Brazil, a young and very beautiful prostitute propositioned me on the beach. She sat down next to me, her red string bikini glowing like hot coals on her coffee-colored skin, and before I could say anything else, I said, "Yes." Never once did I think: You're a heterosexual woman, a banker from New York City. You wear designer suits, dark hose and stylish yet sensible pumps. You carry a black leather briefcase, you lunch at Le Cirque, and the most daring thing you've done in years is wear slingbacks before June. You date expensively dressed men who drink too much and like the true liberated woman you are; you always pay half the check when you go out to dinner.

But I said, "Yes," and I meant it. Fifty dollars for one hour. On the way back to my hotel room, I bought her and myself large rum drinks with extravagant displays of fruit. My limbs were trembling and I was so turned on, I could almost imagine an erection straining against my suit. In fact, I even looked down at myself to make sure I didn't have one. I closed the door to my suite and turned on the radio. She didn't speak English and I didn't speak her language but we both knew what was going to happen. I offered her a cigarette and instead she reached inside her straw bag and handed me a tube of suntan oil. Then she lay down and untied the top of her string bikini. Those breasts! Those nipples, the size and color of copper pennies, already erect! I drank half my drink and squeezed the oil into my hands. I knelt over her and began to massage her half-naked body.

She motioned for me to kiss her and she tasted like salt from the ocean, like honey...she rolled onto her belly and tugged at the bottom of her bikini until it fell away, a scrap of scarlet fabric. I dripped the oil on her back, her thighs, and let it run in rivulets into the crack of her ass. I stood up and pulled my suit off, let it drop to the floor. She rolled over, stood up, completely naked, all bronzed, glorious, gleaming with oil, and seductively wrapped her lips around a slice of orange in her drink. I pulled the orange out of her mouth with my mouth, and suddenly she was all over me. Her tongue darting in my ears, my mouth...I wished I had a cock, completely erect, so I could ram it up inside her. Instead, I pushed her down on the bed and ate her, her greased hips bucking up against my face, then suddenly her fingers were inside me and I came so hard and so strong I practically slid off the edge of the bed, which was completely soaked by now.

She kissed my face, gathered together her string bikini, and disappeared inside the bathroom. I sat on the floor of my hotel room, completely naked, stunned. What had I done?

Who would I tell, if ever? When she reappeared, I handed her fifty dollars, ran my hands through her hair, and asked if I would ever see her again. She smiled because she had no idea what I had said. But I thought, I could get used to this, I really could. I fantasized about bringing her back to New York, making an honest woman of her.

I scanned the beach all the rest of that week, hoping to see her again, wanting desperately to tell her I loved her, but I never saw her until I got to the airport in Rio. There she stood, arm in arm with her husband. The red string bikini safely packed away, she looked and was the wife of a respectable businessman. When she saw me, she winked, threw me a kiss, and boarded the plane.

Top

My biggest problem is that I could never find a top. I mean, there are bottoms for days, for days, man, so I decided to become a top, just like that, overnight, I became one, and I decided one night, for money—why not? So I brought this guy up to my apartment and I put this dog collar around his neck and tied him to the stove and turned on all the flames. And suddenly I found that I was getting off on it. Sort of.

And then I threw twenty-five tomatoes at him.

And this red juice was running down his body and over his really hard…hard…hardness. I mean, this guy was really hung, and suddenly I couldn't hold up this thing anymore, of being the top, that is, and I fell on the floor—I think he loved it—and what could he do, he was totally tied up to the stove, with all the flames going—the room was really, really hot and my nipples were really, really hard, and I took this olive oil and I smeared it all over my pussy, all over my body, and I was dripping wet, and he kept telling me, "Suck me off, suck me off," so I did. I crawled across the floor, incredibly slowly, and then I got to his hard…throbbing…throbbingness. And I sucked him off, really hard, all the way down my throat, I sucked and sucked and sucked until I pulled the jism right out of him, and he came down my throat, and at the last minute I pulled him out of my mouth and he urinated all over my face and my tongue. I licked the last bit of come off the floor and then I leaned back, plunged my fingers inside my pussy, and beat off.

I'm so glad I'm over all that now.

How Does It Feel?

When I walk in the door, he has garlic, anchovies, and olives simmering in hot oil. A plate of greens on the table, Mississippi Delta blues playing on the stereo, a pot of pasta cooking on the stove. The meal is delicious, spicy, the tang of garlic lingering in my mouth, grated cheese over everything. Underneath my black T-shirt, I am wearing a purple lace camisole; under my pants, sheer purple panties. As I suck pasta into my mouth, I feel very sexy. He asks if I want to walk to a neighborhood bar for a drink.

I think, "Yes, one drink and back for sex."

We sit at the bar and play fifty songs on the jukebox. At first it is fun to brush up against him and feel that static electricity, that spark, that happens between two people who know they will be having sex later on, but for now it's just playtime, taut nipples and tight thighs bumping up against knees and elbows. His mouth just inches from mine. I can almost smell his breath, but then he orders another single malt. And then another. And another. I grow weary of the jukebox, the neon, the tourists thronging the bar after the Broadway shows.

He says, "I don't know what it is about you, but I feel so good. Like really good. Like I could sit here all night and drink." I think, "Yes, but not with me."

The inside of his thigh begins to hold less and less appeal as he orders yet another single malt and plays another fifty songs on the jukebox. The garlic has made my mouth dry and so I order a glass of water. I am smoking too many cigarettes and looking at my watch. I calculate how many minutes it will take to get home if I leave now. But I know I can't. My bag is at his apartment.

He leans his head drunkenly into my breast and kisses my neck. I thrill briefly to the imprint of his lips on my skin, but it is too late. A good-looking man and his date enter the bar, and he sits on the empty bar stool next to mine. We exchange glances, he and I, and I do not flinch when he puts his hand on my thigh.

It feels good, it feels really, really good.

My date orders yet another drink. I don't care anymore. This hand on my thigh is much better than the thought of drunken sex. Under cover of darkness, I now put my hand on the man's thigh. His girlfriend chatters away about shopping on Fifth Avenue. Little does she know my hand is in her boyfriend's crotch, his erection growing with each second. I turn slightly and he rubs the back of my ass in slow, slow circles. Our hands are leading separate lives from the rest of our bodies.

I am rubbing your ass in slow, slow circles. I am rolling your erection in my hand like a Cuban cigar.

I drop my cigarettes, and when my head is down I kiss this man's leg. Then I bite his calf. He barely flinches. I know he is smiling. I slide off the barstool and rub up against him. I feel his eyes on me. My drunken date and the preoccupied Long Island princess have no idea what we are doing. Our arms, our legs, our fingers, our eyes have fallen in love. In the bathroom, I fold my business card into a tiny little square and hide it in my pocket. Back at the bar, my date is watching the hockey game and singing along to Bob Dylan. I search out my lover's hand. I leave my name, my address, my phone number in his moist palm. Then I pull my date from the bar stool so we can leave. He is singing, "...How does it feel?"

It feels good, baby. It feels really, really good.

Whack Me Off

We talk about it constantly, and then you turn to me when we get home and say, "I like talking about sex," and I can tell you're stiff, and you grab my hand and put it right on your handle, and you say, "Whack me off, whack me off." I'm a little scared of you. You lean back like an Aryan and say, "Whack me off, whack me off," and I do, and you say, "Faster," like you've just got to come. It's all about your coming quickly, and rather than being a turn-off—like, "Honey, you should just go at my clit for hours first"—I find it sexy that you want to come quickly. Right now. Not another minute can pass. "Whack me off," you say with insistence, virtual desperation, and command in your eyes.

Aviatrix

Remember this as you crash and burn into the hot heart of the Pacific sun with a stranger on your arm. Remember the plight of Icarus, those feathered wings dissolving under a lover's touch, his hands on himself, his pride, the steep plunge to cool himself off, and yes, you are a woman of some prominence, and yes, you hit the sky with the same determination, the same love of the game, but hubris is never rewarded in Greek myths.

And yes, it's intoxicating to play these games with yourself, alone for hours in the cockpit of the Electra: you and your handsome navigator. His eyes are deep and dark, I hear. And when he shoots the stars with an octant for a navigational fix, he projects the lines of latitude and longitude onto your body, your smooth flank, your small breasts, your long legs...the equatorial line straddles the smooth rise of your belly even as it measures the distance between Brazil and Africa, Africa and India, India and Australia, and east, farther east until all you can see is the wide expanse of the Pacific and your warm hands on the throttle of the engine.

And then you finally understand that the earth is like a woman's body, not just your body but every woman's body, the hot flat plains of the desert, the dense equatorial jungle, the undulating coastline, but you realize all this too late. You and your handsome navigator run out of fuel, minutes from Howland Island. I know what you are thinking, but back on earth, you are mortal and married. And you will pay a high price for transcendence, for love, for the romance of flight.

Ask Icarus....

I hear he haunts the wide blue mouth of the Pacific, just east of Howland Island.

White Clogs

"Are you a nurse?"

"No."

"I do S/M."

"That's an interesting way to put it."

"Well...I wasn't an English major."

"How old are you?" She turned and looked at him straight in the eye.

"Twenty-three."

"I'm forty-one," she said and immediately turned back to her work.

A few moments passed in the dark bar before he started in again....

"What are you writing?"

"I'm filling out a patient's report," she lied.

"Oh."

"So what are you?" she asked.

"What do you mean?"

"Dominant or submissive?"

"Both."

He told her not to take him lightly, that he was no idiot, so she asked twenty questions. Where do you live? Where do you work? "Brighton Beach, with my parents. I just graduated from Yeshiva."

This is how it started. He told her how he had developed a foot fetish when he was young, while he was watching a children's program. He said that the show had moved the camera across a line of feet of children from different nations, ethnicities, and colors. Bare toes of different hues. He was only five. But he had masturbated during this episode, and he told her that when he had first walked into the bar, he had noticed that she was wearing white clogs with no socks. And then he asked, "May I hold your foot?" in a voice that sounded like he was playing Dungeons and Dragons.

She slipped her foot out of her clog and he grabbed it and put it on his lap. He was erect. But they kept talking. And then, "May I open my pants?" And he unbuttoned his jeans and put her foot onto his naked erection underneath the table in the dark corner of this dark pub.

When she asked him, "What kind of shoe is your favorite shoe?" he responded, "Anything off."

"You mean unique?"

"No, off the foot," he said.

She is rather conservative when it comes to these things. So when he told her he enjoyed the salty smell and taste of a woman's foot that had been in stockings and pumps all day, and he asked, "You know what I mean?" she had to respond that never in her life had she worn stockings and pumps. In fact, she goes out of her way to choose professions where she doesn't have to wear stockings and pumps.

It was the talk of golden showers in his bathtub at his parents' house in Brighton Beach that vaguely fascinated but mainly horrified her. And then the talk of shit. Well, she changed the subject quickly, and he asked if her nipples were hard and good for clamps, and he stood up from across the table and sat right next to her—like the dirty old man that he already was at the age of twenty-three. And she, behaving like the little girl that she insisted on being at the age of forty-one, obliged—lifted her shirt and showed him her hard pink nipples, and he responded happily but kept on talking about this and that and about S/M and the clubs, and then she thought, "Yes, yes, yes, yes, how you flog, yes, the superiority of a multiple hitting device like the cat-o'-nine tails over the riding crop, but what about spanking?" And she asked that out loud.

And he reluctantly said, "Well, yes."

And she asked, "How about here?"

And he said, "I can't really do it properly," as he started to bend her over his knee.

"No, not over your knee," she said. "I'll move my ass just so, and you hit me while I sit."

"Oh, the bossy submissive," he said as his hand came down like a master on her ass—immediately painting a smile across her face.

He wore a backward baseball cap, his grandparents were from the Ukraine, and he had a hand like God that came down fifteen times, full force, and pounded her across the table. He put his face close to hers, and she noticed for the first time how he looked. Beautiful.

One Man Made Love to Me

One man made love to me on a balcony thirty stories up, overlooking the East River. He slid my black linen trousers down around my ankles while his lips caressed the nape of my neck, while his legs slid back and forth between my legs. And then he played "Claire de Lune" on the piano while I lay like an odalisque in the living room. I was completely naked and the lights from the bridge illuminated the room. Later, later, I swam up from deep, deep sleep and abruptly announced I needed to go home. He stood up in the darkness and said,

"Stop acting like a man." I said, "Walk me down to a cab." He said, "No."

On my way home at four in the morning, crossing the bridge over the dark waters of the river, I smiled, desperately happy to be going home, alone.

Another man made love to me after drinking half a bottle of Scotch and then had a nervous breakdown, naked, in the middle of his own bed, because I wanted to go home. Because I said:

"I don't sleep with strangers, I'm sorry."

He walked into the kitchen, his penis bobbing up and down, and guzzled cold water from a bottle. I smiled when I saw this and he got even crazier, demanded half the money he spent on dinner. So I took another cab, smiling again to myself in the darkness, a river of semen dripping down my legs at three in the morning.

Spanish Harlem

He lay across my lap like The Pietà, except he was facing down, screwing me, his beautiful ass in my hands. Almost a child. He had insisted, with his stupid blue eyes, that I go into the next room, take off all my clothes, turn out the light, and get in bed. He came in and immediately entered me, then squirmed to this position, where his ass—gorgeous—was in my palm. Enough so that I ran my hand across the skin and slapped it until it was red.

He told me he screwed girls hanging them out the window five stories above crack addicts. He told me that he didn't want to know my marital status and that if he hadn't already known my name, he wouldn't want to know that, either, as he pulled my arms behind my back and threw me down in Spanish Harlem.

Getting it on with him was not half as good as the way he curled in my arms all night long, held on to me like a child (I was at least a foot taller than he) as I eyed, in my half-sleep, still aroused, the boxing bag hanging in the middle of his bedroom, just a few feet from the bed, and I twisted his nipple in his sleep. He rolled over and practically started sucking his thumb.

He said that he imagined he had a vagina, that he beat off with his blinds up, and that he drew stick figures—dirty pictures—that he masturbated to. He also showed me his acrylic abstract "art" paintings, which I tried desperately to obliterate from my mind every time we got it on. He looked into my eyes and told me what hot shit he was, and how he wanted me dead.

He had no mind, a tiny prick, the chest of an Adonis, curls like the David, and an honorable discharge from the Marines.

His hands squeezed my neck and he pushed me down and told me, "Don't be nice or I'll stop screwing you. I'll leave you if you're ever nice to me." And I one-upped him: out of bed, I told him I was not interested in anything about him but screwing him, and then he looked hurt. I said I didn't want to be friends. I didn't want to get together for coffee and discuss his poetry. No. "That's not the point, is it, when you're a hot-shit screw like you. If you're going to be a sadist, be a goddamn sadist, for Christ's sake," I whispered as he ran away from me in the rain, on the Upper West Side, the day I stopped slapping and cupping his gorgeous, gorgeous ass.

Officer Sanchez

The gun is blue, cold steel, it glints like silver in the light of the full moon. It flashes heavily in his hands before he rams it up against my temple. Then I feel like laughing. This can't be real. He is young, very young, a budding sociopath saying, "Give me all your fucking money, you fucking bitch, or I'll blow your fucking head off."

I turn to smile at him. A quick trip to the deli for cigarettes has turned into this. I counted out quarters before I left because I had no money, literally. Minutes later I find myself in the hands of this kid brandishing a silver gun in the moonlight. I say, "I have no money. I have nothing." I gesture to my costume, black overcoat, red flannel pajamas, $12.99 at the local discount store. Ha, ha, ha. Look at me. Do I look like I have money? He repeats his "fucking bitch" speech. I tell him again, "I have no money."

He cocks the trigger, and in response I lose my peripheral vision. It's not funny anymore. My head floats over my body. I have no money. I have no money. He grabs my hand and demands my gold jewelry. But, alas, I am wearing silver. I apologize profusely, over and over. And then I turn and walk away. Calmly, quietly. I say to myself, "I'll call 911 when I get home."

When Officer Sanchez enters my apartment, he's at least six feet tall. Delicious black eyes. I picture him ramming his cock up inside me. "Is that what you want, lady?" And I say, "Yes, yes, yes."

While he's taking notes, all I can think about is his gun and badge strewn across my bed. First his cock is in my mouth, then his gun. Down at the precinct, I flip through mug shots, but I am acutely conscious of his legs, tightly swathed in blue polyester. Then I look at his ass: it is pure perfection. Back at home, I alternate between the surreal movie of the kid, the silver gun, the moonlight, and Officer Sanchez letting me have it...right where it counts...right between my legs. I alternate between ecstasy and absolute fear. That night I dream that I am Officer Sanchez, with a large cock, and that I fuck women indiscriminately: Black women, white women, Latina women. They're all beautiful, they all have such beautiful tits, and they all take me inside them with little gasps of pleasure. I am in charge, I have the power, I have the gun—fully cocked and loaded.

PART VII

When I Kiss You, Your Mouth Is Filled

Flute

Floating through my window to your window, the sound of the bathtub running. We've got our agreement that when you hear the pipes rattle and the hot water spitting into my clawfoot, you will open your kitchen window and, through the chicken wire that prevents your cat from jumping out across the air shaft into my apartment, your lips and tongue will begin their thumping on the mouth of your flute. The sounds are crazy and screaming and they move fast up and down the scales as the water beats down on me, my legs spread up on the green tile. And while I'm listening, my eyes are wide open to the orgy you've painted on my ceiling, and the love affair we have that is never spoken or acknowledged, flute and bath.

I Want a Man

I want a man who's so hot for me he'll jump through a ring of fire to get into my pants. I want a man who's so hot for me he'll fly out of an airplane minus a parachute and land in the middle of my bed. I want a man who's so hot for me he'll cover my naked body with rose petals gathered from the four corners of the earth from roses so rare they grow only high up in the mountains where the air is so thin and the birds fly so high his life is constantly in danger but he doesn't care because he's so hot for me he'll die for me. I want a man who's so hot for me money is no object. I want a man who's so hot for me nothing's too good for me. I want a man who's so hot for me so hot for me so hot for me that my mouth is a temple my heart is a cathedral and my cunt is his home.

Tit in Mouth, Ear to Wall

My ear was to the wall, his prick was in her pussy. The bed coils sprang as I popped my own cherry, squeezing and climaxing again and again. Squeak, squeak, "Oh, oh!"

Another wall, another year, on Gramercy Park, the Asian chick with the two big dogs every Sunday morning like clockwork—a low "Oh, oh, oh, oh," rhythmically building until "Oh! Oh! Yes! Yes!" The dogs barking. My fingers in my cunt, my orgasm against the wall through my mouth—whispered—thinking of the dogs licking her snatch.

Another wall, three years earlier, in a Carolina condo—every afternoon at four, I opened my window and heard her getting screwed, white trash fucking as I closed my blinds and muffled the vibrator against clit and blanket, beating off to this bitch call.

Ten Thousand Volts of Electricity

I want a prescription for Valium, Librium, and cocaine. And then I want ten thousand volts of electricity shot through my skull so I'll forget everything. I want Freud, Jung, and Miller to screw me and every TV talk-box idiot to write my life story on the back of a pack of matches, sell it for a quarter on the corner where they sell dime bags of pot. I want long black hair, red lipstick, high heels dug into the small of my back. I want a black man and a white woman to tongue me to death and ten thousand volts of electricity shot hot up to my pussy. Hook me up to a socket, wire me, brain me, shock me.

I want to walk the West Side piers at midnight, pick up a man dressed like a woman, and suck his dick till he shoots his universe, smears his lipstick like death. Wire me, brain me with ten thousand volts, dress me in green and read to me:

"He maketh me to lie down, he maketh me live through life like death, like electricity."

I wanna smoke crack, Jack. Smoke it through my ass, Jack. Smoke it, Jack. Smoke me. Smoking from ten thousand volts of e-lec-tric-i-ty. E-lec. Tric-i-ty. Titty. I want to dance the dance Salome danced, want Herod between my legs, want the head of

John the Baptist, want to suck Christ's tits on the cross: hear him moan, beg for mercy. And then I say:

"Baby, I ain't got no mercy. All I got is ten thousand volts. Good enough for you. Good enough for me. You hot now? You smoking now, Jack? I say, 'You smoking now, Jack?' Good Jack. Good boy. Ten thousand volts, and you ain't whistling Dixie."

Seven in the Morning

The moment your black-haired bitch laughed on my periphery with her hysterical and cruel smile, I turned to you and noticed, for the first time, your teeth. I thought about running my tongue along the landscape of your mouth and knew I could never socialize with you and your wife again. Your fingers on the table suddenly turned to penises, you sucked cigarettes, slicing basil for pesto you would serve your wife the next day, you talked of the Holocaust and gesticulated constantly. Your wife then excused herself and went to bed in a blur of Scotch, leaving us at the kitchen table at four in the morning, when the fifteen minutes before the first kiss turned into five years. Because one day your wife stood at the elevator—with her cat in a cage—and never came back, plummeting me onto the window seat at a downtown bar where you leapt at me and turned me into dust. "Your place or my place," your erection dancing on the bar, saying, "Come home with me and I'll blow into your mouth like the wind, I'll make your eyes fill with stars," lettuce dropping from your fingers into my mouth and your nails running up my thigh, cognac dripping slowly down my throat, and we swooped home into your extramarital bed as the sun rose, and you threw off your clothes and dove into me. At seven in the morning.

Ultra-Delicious

Your tongue travels down my belly slowly, slowly. Your teeth disentangle my jeans from my body, your tongue dismembers my underwear. Your hands unloose my breasts from their tight, pink bondage. And you're hard, and your cock is long and thick, log-jamming my cunt with no hope of tomorrow. My pussy is wet and glistening because your tongue spent an eternity harrowing the wet fields of wheat.

I'm not even breathing now—I am gasping for breath, gasping in pleasure—electricity shoots through my body. The sky goes dark, the roots of the trees dig in, the animals run for shelter, the rain shatters the roofs of the houses while my white body writhes underneath your desire. Your fingernails are needles that rake the virgin landscape of my back.

My tongue begins to speak a language so foreign only your cock seems to understand, so I crawl down and quietly slip the tip into the back of my throat. In retaliation, your fingers dredge the swamp of my cunt. I shed my skin and float into your mouth like a moth crashing into a porch light.

My hipbones are bruised, my face is rubbed raw. And by God, you're a man on the threshold of glory, on the verge of a heart attack.

My own breathing becomes so labored and yet so quiet. I am slipping into shock. Then the tide runs in and the rivers flood and we are at it again: fucking as if our lives depended on it. We swim past the buoys and mile markers, ignoring the sharks and the poisonous incandescent coral.

Then my cunt explodes and a milky universe shoots across your face. A small galaxy of glowing planets and red stars collide with the bones in your body. You moan, "It's like death, it's like death," while my middle finger engages your ass in silky, military maneuvers: a covert mission of espionage.

That's right, baby: It's like taking a ride on a roller coaster, on a toboggan in the dead of winter. Hold on and hold tight, and for God's sake don't look at the scenery. Scream your brains out, but save the tears for later.

"Yes, yes, yes," you sob.

I am waxed clean and every pore in my body swims in saltwater and come. We have become messengers of light and death. Saints of unsurpassable sanctity. Unable to breathe or disentangle the mass of our flesh. You are woman and I am man. What your cock has joined together, let no ideology tear asunder.

"Yes, yes, yes," you sob.

In my winged, saintly glory, I wring out warm towels and dribble water onto your ravaged back, over the dark curling hairs on your legs, around the clenched fingers of your fist, into the fresh minnows swimming between my legs.

Our breathing becomes even and deep as we pass into sleep and onto a windswept plain where the sky is so low and so purple we pass like shadows through every cloud. Your strong legs curl heavily around mine, and small angels the size of snowflakes pass through our skin like water passes through the earth.

Tattoos

I want to sweep aside all friendship, as if I was taking all the unpaid traffic tickets from your dashboard and throwing them out the window. And I want to sit on top of you in your truck at the red light, I want to look into your eyes and forget you're my friend and run my hand up the butter-olive of your ridiculous macho tattoos and then just slip you inside me and kiss you and close my eyes so I don't know it's you. Then I want you to plaster your tattoos on my body, love me so close that I take them on. I want all your women smeared all over my body in blue and red, and I want to be a Latino with a truck and a cell phone. I want the hard muscles and the push-ups, and the jet-black hair that is almost blue, and all the girls to want me. And when the tattoos become mine, I want them to wiggle for me, I want them to speak to me quietly and be my friends. I want the women to spring to life and do a holy strip show for me in a darkened room with a red velvet curtain in North Beach, where they used to dance flamenco. I want one of your women to pour red wine into my mouth, and your mother to give me a loaf of bread. I want your daughter to do a belly dance as I squirm and push you inside me—until it hurts—and we press the years of friendship out of our skulls, and finally fall in love.

Poet

No muse could possibly be more erotic or more cruel than the poetic muse. So she is trapped, lusting harder and longer for this muse than she ever did for her tall husband, that sexy, handsome man with his leonine shock of lazy hair who created an electric current in her body that left her wide-eyed, her fingertips blue, her hair smoking. He bit her when they made love, he bit her and made her bleed, and he drank her blood and told her how sweet it tasted on his ruby lips.

But then he betrayed her like she always knew he would. He left her for a more grounded woman. And now it is November, and she is alone, and she wonders if she can possibly survive until early spring, when the blood will rush to her loins again, when the trees will drip with fat white blossoms, because that is the only time that this muse possesses her, fills her.

Meanwhile, it is still early winter in London, and she is alone, no muse, no husband, and her children are sleeping. So she slides her hands into her woolen pants and the shock of her cold hands on her warm moist cunt creates a storm cloud over her head, an electrical storm that climaxes in a milky spray of vowels, consonants, and metaphors that barely sustain her into the next day.

On the Phone

On the answering machine, "Are you there, are you there?" His very large cock implanted in my cheeks, I held the muscles in the back of my throat so as not to gag on his hugeness. His clothes were still on, only the zipper unzipped, and me—with only a nipple and half a pussy out for him to manipulate like a genius with one hand—the clit, the ass, and the gal. Then this guy fucked me as, in my mind, I walked down the streets I grew up on and I tried to find my way home from school. His girlfriend's voice called out on the answering machine—"Are you there, are you there, are you there?"—half crying as he pressed his hand on my mouth and shoved himself deeper inside me. When he came, he always kept it from me, coming into either a prophylactic or his own hand. He closed his mouth, too, hiding his pleasure as if his girlfriend was waiting and listening outside the door. But we knew exactly where she was, as we screwed to the pleading song of her voice, its masochistic wail on the phone, voicing my orgasm as he covered my mouth.

Junkie Lover

I want to be your junkie. I want to be your drug. I want to be your dark whore, your dark horse. Your scar where the saber severed your skin in two, the twisted magenta flesh that reminds you just how sweet life can really be—I am your demon lover come to call; I want to be your lover baby. I want to be your girl.

I want you to detox in a clinic after spending one night with me. I want you to stand on a street corner at three o'clock in the morning begging strangers for my address, my phone number, and then I want you to howl like a rabid wolf underneath my bedroom window, your cock so swollen, so engorged with blood, it is painful for you to climb the fire escape to my bedroom window.

But you do, and I let you, I let you climb in because I want to be your lover, baby. I want to be your girl. You'll be Lawrence of Arabia, the desert sheik. And I'll be your horse, your poppy, your coca leaf, your needle, the silver spoon where you cook up your wildest wet dreams. I'll come to you at night while you're sleeping and wrestle your wrists and your ankles to the bedposts with purple silk because I want to be your lover, baby. I want to be your girl.

And after I am done with you, you'll be back for more. I'll cook up another batch of my love and pump it through a syringe: Pull back your shirt sleeve, tighten the tourniquet around your arm, open up your veins with the hollow tip of the needle

and

and

inject my sweet sweet self deep into the blood of you. Because I want to be your lover, baby. I want to be your girl.

In the Bardo

In the Bardo, in *The Tibetan Book of the Dead,* deep in the life you fall into, deep in the still water you fall fall into, small devils plague you, bite at your skin. Small devils that become angels when you befriend them. Deep in the Bardo, when you fall out of life, when you end your life and fall fall into it, when you take a deep plunge, take a deep breath and never let it out, when you spread your red wings, when you sail across a dark forest, when you swim, swim, swim into a river lit only by the stars, into a room inhabited only by the moon. When you paint pictures of the universe with primary colors.

When you made love to a man for two hours. When you did him in a dark room with no light. You screwed him and you screwed him. He slid his fingers inside your mouth. He slid his tongue into your ear and he is deep deep deep inside you but you can't see him in the dark room; you hear only yourself say, "Oh, my God. I like that. I really do." And when he asks to make love to you in the bright light, you hear yourself say, "I can't. I can't do that." But you roll over onto his chest and feel dark coils of dark hair curling up against your thighs and a slick river of sweat falling, falling from his forehead, and he is a stranger, but it doesn't matter to you.

Deep in the Bardo, in the afterlife, you lose your body. You float out of your body, but you are still you. It is strange how this happens. It is strange how this feels: this disconnection from your body, the way devils become angels when you lose your fear of life, when you fall out of death and into the dark river.

Now it is midnight and he enters you again. And your legs start to ache because you carry them over your head so he can penetrate you deeper and harder, so he can strike gold, so he can get at the source of the river, at the warm hot center of your womb, and you smile in the dark but it doesn't matter because he can't see you and he can't hear you. After he has screwed you for the third time, he lights a candle in a coconut shell, and the warm wax floats with a solitary light.

And the beach is silver in the moonlight, but you are not cold, and the stars are brilliant and when your demons come to call, you know them all, you have made love to them, you have seen the inside of their red eyes, and you are not afraid. You invite them to come inside you, and they come inside you. In the Bardo, in the afterlife, when you fall out of life, they come inside you, they become angels, and then they rest inside your womb.

Baptism

I could move to Tibet and hang prayer flags along the icy slopes of the mountains and light incense in gleaming brass pots. I could summon my totem, the hawk, and have it circle the mountains as I meditate. Or I could take a shower with you. And watch the hot water travel down your naked body. I could stand next to you and soap up your body. I'd start with your face, your arms, and move down to your genitals, but not until I have placed them, like rare fruit, inside my mouth. You whisper in my ear, "Don't stop." And the bathroom is lit with candles and the hot shower fills the room with blue clouds of blue steam, and it is like we are in the jungle and you are a tropical bird that I have captured in my mouth. And in my arms. Your feathered wings are the colors of lapis and malachite. They unfurl around me. And when I kiss you, your mouth is filled with water and washes all the sins from our naked bodies.

ERIN CRESSIDA WILSON is a critically acclaimed and internationally produced playwright and screenwriter. She has been honored by the NEA, the Rockefeller Foundation and the California Arts Council. Her plays are published by Smith & Kraus.

LILLIAN ANN SLUGOCKI has been developing and writing award-winning programs in radio, television and theater for over fifteen years for such venues as NPR, The Public Theatre, Naked Angels, New Georges, and in Cannes, Edinburgh and London.